DAWN GARISCH (Harare, 1958) is an author and medical doctor. She is founding member of the Life Righting Collective. She has published seven novels, two collections of poetry, short stories, a non-fiction work and a memoir. She has produced five plays and a short film, and has written for television. Her poem 'Blood Delta' won the DALRO prize (2007); 'Trespass' was shortlisted for the Commonwealth Prize in Africa (2010); 'Miracle' won the EU Sol Plaatje Poetry Award (2011); and 'What to Do About Ricky' won the Short.Sharp.Stories competition (2013). Her novel *Accident* was longlisted for the Barry Ronge *Sunday Times* Fiction Award (2018) and *Breaking Milk* was shortlisted for the *Sunday Times* South Africa/ CNA Fiction Award (2021). In 2023 she published her first collection of short stories, *What Remains*.

BREAKING MILK

Dawn Garisch

HÉLOÏSE
PRESS

First published in Great Britain in 2024 by
Héloïse Press Ltd
4 Pretoria Road
Canterbury CT1 1QL

www.heloisepress.com

© Dawn Garisch

Published by arrangement with Karavan Press via Catrina Wessels Rights Management
Originally published by Karavan Press in 2019 in South Africa

Cover design by Laura Kloos
Edited by Karina M. Szczurek
Offset by Tetragon, London
Printed and bound in Great Britain by CPI Group (UK) Ltd, Croydon, CR0 4YY

The moral right of Dawn Garisch to be identified as the author of this work has been asserted in accordance with the Copyrights, Designs and Patents Act, 1988.

All rights reserved. Except as otherwise permitted under current legislation, no part of this publication may be reproduced or transmitted in any form or by any means, electronic or mechanical, including photocopy, recording, or any information storage and retrieval system, without permission in writing from the publisher.

ISBN 978-1-7397515-8-6

This book is a work of fiction. Any resemblance to names, characters, organisations, places and events is entirely coincidental.

To the future

BREAKING MILK

Kate wakes earlier than usual; it is still dark. There was rain in the night, pitting against the window pane. Also a terrible dream; the residue lies heavily in her belly, yet she can't locate what evoked this. How easily a dream's edge slips away.

The rain roused her round two. She lay still for a long while, tied to the loop of anxious thought about the knife-edge today's surgery will bring, dividing life into the time before and the time after, not knowing which way things will fall.

She imagined Jess also sleepless in the dark, the two of them so far apart. Her daughter would be sitting beside the hospital cot, wrenched endlessly awake, holding a wretched vigil over her sons.

Everybody needs another to watch over them with interest and concern, she thought. A guardian, a witness, a comforter. There is much to be said for a benevolent eye.

The cut of Jess's words on the phone last week when she gave her mother the operation date: Don't come. Two severing words pushing her away, like the palm of a hand in her face. Don't come. All possible reasons for this have filed past Kate, convicting her of her deficiencies.

Kate's mind switches to another son, Luzoko, in pain, waiting for healing. Tonight was his first wet one out in the wild, thankfully not too cold. Those young men have only a blanket each and a makeshift shelter.

Luzoko's mother also struggles to sleep in her home near the mountain, arriving at work tired-eyed. Nosisi says she is proud of her son, but she also suffers.

So many women down the ages, Kate reflects, have lain awake in the earth's great shadow, insomniac over their progeny, their sons and daughters intent on escaping their mothers' intractable worry.

The dream! Kate remembers now, as vividly as a movie: Jessica, as a young girl, drowning in the dam. Her halo of blonde hair was wafting about her head, her blue eyes stared blankly. One arm angled to the side, trailing. The water that had closed over her was a deep, palmiet brown, suffused by shredded light. Kate was standing above, on the jetty perhaps, the surface shivering in the wind, blurring Jess's features. Kneeling, she reached her arm down into the cold and gripped the child by her hip, grabbing the hard edge of her pelvic bone, her fingers sinking into the soft give of her belly. Even though she pulled with all her might, the water held her daughter like glue. Afraid she would be dragged in after her, Kate let go, and watched her daughter sink out of sight.

The dream is a tangle of panic in her belly. Reason lifts her like a lifejacket: It is superstitious to consider dreams prophetic.

A pointless torment. Jessica could swim by the age of three. Kate brought her daughter to the farm during the holidays and taught her to swim in the dam. She wanted Jess to know where milk comes from, how to dig for earthworms in the cow turd mud, and to know what the night sky looks like, unobscured by the glow of city lights.

Her severed daughter, an unsaved child.

Children should never die, she thinks, as she lies listening for any movement from the room above. That is to say, children should never die before their parents. Storm and Sky. Such hopeful, hopeless, useless names! Joined names, names that need each other to survive.

There is a stillness, all around, abnormally so. Kate has never heard such silence. As though all creatures, even the elements, are waiting. Holding their breath.

As though the world has exhaled for the last time.

She opens her eyes, struck by the thought: Da! Could her father be dead?

Life is never that considerate.

He must be asleep, finally. Several times in the night Kate heard his intermittent shuffling and banging upstairs, accompanied by Elihle's muffled placating. Her father's stumblings around his room enact his thoughts – aimless, agitated, trapped in the chamber of his skull.

There were nights when he'd barged into Kate's bedroom, until she took to locking her door. Nowadays, he doesn't even come downstairs to try the handle. Perhaps Elihle locks him up in his own bedroom to protect me, Kate surmises. Them up, rather, for Elihle is on the same side of the door. Elihle, dear boy.

For now, they sleep. Today she will not fret about Da and what is to be done in that department.

She hears the soft pulse of an owl's hoot.

She must get up and face her shame: Her daughter does not want her. There is recoil at her centre; she cannot live with this disgrace. Kate knows that she must go over. This is the circumstance that permits her to cross the distance her daughter has put between them three years back.

If Kate had managed to stay married, perhaps none of this would have happened, she worries. After her parents' divorce, Jess had started and then dropped out of two courses. During that turbulent time, Kate had entered the bathroom one morning and was shocked to see a bird in flight tattooed between her daughter's lovely breasts. Soon afterwards, Jess left for London, began working in bars and fell pregnant during a brief affair. Gave birth to twins, and if that wasn't hard enough, they were conjoined at the head. Bad luck, one might call it, or else a chain of poor decisions leading to this disaster.

Why don't you understand, her mother wants to impress upon her, that your life choices thus far leave you very vulnerable. You have nothing, nothing but the dole to fall back on. Gone are the days when a husband or a god would save you.

Surely, Kate worries, there comes a time for a mother to intervene, to insist: Let me in! Let me help you. No matter what the outcome of the surgery today, much will need to be done. She must test whether Jess's intransigence is stronger than her mother's will.

Kate resolves to scrape together her dwindling courage and resources. She will apply a brave smile, and bite back her anger at how life has turned out. Go over to England and help with the aftermath of the surgery, and with her daughter's choices and circumstances, then return to her own broken mess.

Leonard will be there, standing between her and their child. She is not ready to face him, nor the possibility of a new female attachment.

Kate lies with her forearms crossed uncomfortably over her belly. She pinches and pulls at the loose pouches of her elbows. Her skin is coming away in old folds.

There is an ache, insisting, insinuating itself. Something vital inside her is broken, something that needs urgent attention, in an emergency room, say. If she had a broken bone or was vomiting blood, she would be rushed off immediately to a specialist. But she does not display such evidence. Not even a post-mortem would reveal a lesion, even though it is unquestionably a physical sensation, a forked and cored dread that has taken up residence behind her sternum, inserted behind the edge of her ribs. It can only be seen on a PET scan – her pain incandescent, lighting up a region in the limbic area of the brain.

Leonard was the first to inform her that not everyone experiences emotional pain as a physical sensation. He explained, in the days when they were still talking to each other, that his was more of a mental anguish. Kate struggled to understand what her husband was saying, shocked that their perceptions were so different.

Making love, for example. The sensation of coming together, in all meanings of the phrase, was probably an illusion. That time in the garden under a full moon when they were still trying to mend their marriage: Her body was so willing, so open. She thought he'd understood, that they had spliced a real connection, an intimate twining of disparate threads into a reliable cable of love, of intention, one you could commit your whole life to. But she misplaced the full weight of her trust. She failed to reach him.

There is a tumult in her throat – a sob, even a wail, threatening. It is terrifying, she panics: this alienation, this delusion of at-one-ness.

She has not returned Leonard's calls, so she doesn't know his plans. Jess has no doubt invited him.

The grief is not contained within her rib cage.

It suffuses into her legs, making them weak and in danger of imminent collapse, even when lying down. Kate has seen movies where women fell to the ground on hearing terrible news, and has dismissed this as melodramatic. She knows now, distress can attack the back of the knees, dividing the fibre that keeps the body emotionally and physically upright.

Kate lies very still, despite the cramp in her neck, not wanting to move and thereby break open the shell of the new day. A day that must then be lived with all consequences following, stringing themselves together into one long necklace that tightens.

Time behaves so mischievously, paradoxically, she ponders. Like a river that flows backwards. When one is a child, time is wide, expansive, and slow; but as one grows older, time quickens and narrows, rushing, a rapid that hurries to its source to be soaked back into nothing. Strange how the fleeting time of the aged and the tardy time of the child are able to walk together side-by-side: a grandmother with her grandchild.

Kate wills events to halt for one prolonged moment, for plans to freeze over right down to bedrock, so that she can catch her breath, so that they can all stop, stop, and again reconsider the options. Storm and Sky.

Such tiny, vulnerable bodies, such soft, new skin.

Outside it is so dark, it must still be overcast. Scientists say that night is the absence of light, but any poet knows that is not true. Darkness is made of its own substance, it has a presence; right now, it seethes and sidles at her window. Pre-dawn has its own growing tension, awaiting the advent of the morning sunlight that is hurtling towards the farm, racing towards the eastern horizon from the other side of the world, flicking eyes open and intentions on.

Kate reaches out, finds the cord to the bedside lamp and presses the switch. The illumination reveals the Africa-shaped stain on the ceiling above her bed from the time her father left the bathroom taps on upstairs. Africa, her beloved, demented continent.

Caesar and Brutus scrabble and clatter up from their corner at the first signs of movement, eager for the new day. They present their great heads for a stroke and a scratch, their tails whipping up enthusiasm.

Her friend Sharon maintains there are two kinds of thoughts – horizontal thoughts and vertical ones. Garnering her will, Kate tests this, pushing herself upright. The ache shifts slightly but does not let up. Kate decides: A mother never recovers after the separation from her child, the miraculous being that once resided within her body cavity, who fed upon her blood and milk.

On Wilhelm's farm next door, when the newborn calves are herded together and penned away from their mothers, Kate can hear the cows bellowing all day, calling and calling for their young, their udders swollen, their milk stolen for human consumption. It lasts three days, the grief-infused lowing, and then the cow mothers stop. They give up, seeming to accept their lot. Who knows where their sorrow goes.

Kate treats her goats more kindly. The kids stay with their mothers for six weeks, and are slowly separated and weaned, while the milking ensures that the she-goats continue to produce.

Her dogs are her darlings now, she comforts herself, these resilient animals that press at her knees and will never leave her until death takes them.

A sound arrives; a chord resonates, displacing Kate's malaise. Another, and another, until her mind reverberates and lifts with musical phrases. The melody is very familiar, yet Kate cannot place it, nor can she bear to continue with its evocation. It has her mother in it, the woman she wounded with her being.

She banishes the music and slips on her watch. Her feet reach out, feeling for her slippers, her right Achilles stiff and complaining. She stands, pulling a gown around her. Unlocking her bedroom door with an easy twist of the wrist, Kate limps through to the kitchen, releasing light with flicks of switches, the dogs trotting ahead expectantly.

Tea. The room fills with the cadence of water coming to the boil. Such a soothing sound.

Through the window to the east, there is still no sign of the separation of land from sky with the early spill of light. It is not quite half-past four.

Caesar and Brutus wind around her, their soft, pleading eyes embedded in huge heads, their muscular torsos alive with anticipation, awaiting breakfast. While her tea brews, Kate deposits pellets, clattering, into their bowls. Too late, she sees that a long string of ants is back, but she can't be bothered with them right now. The dogs eat anything and don't seem to notice the formic acid relish. They chomp and gulp and their breakfast disappears.

The phone crouches silently on the pile of unopened bills on the table. It is far too early to ring anyone. Jess. Or Sharon. Or the travel agent.

Kate has half an hour to herself. She opens the tin with the golden sailing ship on the lid, a relic from her childhood, and selects a rusk. With her tea, she goes to sit on the stoep. A predawn breeze is stirring. Above, a strip of deep indigo strewn with a bright gravel of stars appears through a rent in the black fabric of cloud.

Round the lamp above the door, three geckoes are poised like crocodiles at a waterhole. They await their prey, muggies and moths that flicker and flit, in and out, drinking pure light. The porch light floods the stoep, then spills down the steps and onto the vague shapes of bush either side of the path, dissipating into the darkness surrounding the house.

The frogs down by the stream, and the cicadas, have resumed their chorus. Kate wonders whether they really ceased their interminable ode to the night at the time she woke. Perhaps she imagined that terrible silence, like the mute sound of the dead, her ears stoppered up with fright.

Far away, strangers will wake shortly to begin preparations. A nurse will lay out instruments – bright slices of steel on a green towelled tray. The reporters, rising, will polish their camera lenses, keen to document the misfortune for the world to see. The grotesque or the bizarre confers instant fame.

Kate's grandchildren are asleep, unaware of what will soon befall them, what has been planned for them in other people's brains. She bites a shred of skin on her lip, mulling: Before they are picked apart, do they share dreams? Can they read each other's thoughts, such as they are at sixteen months old? Do they sense – in the way the first bleach in the night sky at the horizon heralds the blaze of a new day – an impending brazen change?

Her mind is back, feeding at that seething trough.

Thoughts are not like clouds, no matter what the lyrics say; they are more like burrs that cling, obstinately, hooking deeply into the soft substance of the heart.

These rusks are not a good batch. Nosisi has forgotten or exceeded some ingredient. No doubt because she was not concentrating, her mind on her last-born and how well he will survive his initiation. To think: These failed rusks are a product of the misfiring of Nosisi's brain. Every part of our bodies is represented in different areas of our brains. Every aspect of our lives is connected to a thought process, or absence thereof. The whole world is invisibly wired to both human solicitude and imprudence.

Brain surgeons' brains can fail, Kate frets. Concentration can falter, hands can slip. She hopes that surgeons sleep soundly before rising to perform an unusual task requiring a chain of on-the-spot decisions. If they are in the middle of a divorce, or concerned about the welfare of their children, it can affect their judgement. She wonders whether they ask another realm for help as they chew on their breakfasts.

Today, neurosurgeons will attempt to fix that which was made broken. A battle of the gods will be fought over the anaesthetised bodies of her grandsons.

There is the Cape grassbird's rousing call, playing off another's, and the sunbird's, with its sugary warbling. And there: a dove's throb. The whitening sky calls Kate to her rounds, as does the rambunctious cock announcing the day; also the sound of Gert from the paddock, calling the animals to the milking hok.

Gradually the world is taking shape in the weak morning light.

Caesar and Brutus leap up as one and bound down the steps towards the hedge, sending a volley of barks out ahead of them. Kate leans forward, trying to see what they are after. Probably a porcupine, come to grub up arums. She hopes Brutus has learnt his lesson after she had to extract five long spines from his head last summer.

The days rotate, everything remains the same.

Everything will change forever.

Suddenly, Kate is sick of tea, after relishing it every morning her whole life. It does not satisfy, it leaves her mouth dry. She tosses the remainder into a bush and goes inside. Pressure of the bladder.

There is damp coming through the wall next to the toilet. Kate appreciates the fact that nature endlessly reclaims its own, crumbling structures back into the soil, with humans resisting the inevitable, shoring up their construct of the world. She admires nature's quiet persistence, except that this is her own house.

Poor us, she ponders. Ultimately, we cannot win. Eventually the systems that prevent our bodies merging with the landscape will fail.

Her father had dealt with these structural deteriorations when his mind was still capable of issuing commands in an appropriate sequence for his body to follow, involving a complex interplay of recall, planning, volition, action and follow through. These operations used to be simple, ordinary, and everyone took such abilities for granted. Gert would help him, this too was a given. Now, Da's incapacity has evoked Gert's resistance. Infuriatingly, he is no longer willing to assist around the house.

I will mention the damp again, she resolves, and watch him closely to discern whether he has not attended to the problem because of forgetfulness or stubbornness. It is pointless locking horns with him, old goat. The man who was her mentor now sees her as minor. Inferior. Woman.

Perhaps he is merely tired.

She picks up her old jeans from where they lie sprawled on the washing basket. They will do, she reasons. Pointless pulling on clean clothes to attend to this kind of life. Kate, too, is turning into a goat, trailing the pungent odour, identifying with their hard, ebullient hairiness.

She schloffs through to the kitchen, switching off lights. At the back door, she sheds the slippers and slides her feet into her boots. Turns on the radio. The five o'clock weather report announces partially clouded skies and scattered showers, then serves up fragments of news – headlines, they call them. Another corruption scandal, Kate fumes. These politicians are like naughty children lying to their mothers, their fingers crossed behind their backs, thinking they can get away with it.

Another flood in China. Fires sparked by severe drought in Australia. The world, tilting towards ongoing disaster.

Again the telephone catches her eye. It squats, black and plastic, this portal to the world, to Jess. The open wound of hurt children. A headache clamps the back of her neck; vertigo starts up, with no one to hold on to.

Her daughter should have come home when she first fell pregnant, Kate mourns. London is such a terrible place to bring up babies. Jess was born there one winter while Leonard was on sabbatical. The old mother country, England, with its bleak sky's incessant dribble, is a myth that those who live in former colonies should let go of – the home of fairytales, mad spelling and roast beef. Doesn't Jess know, we are Africans now. We are of this blood, this earth. Yet the home she'd created here with Leonard was trashed by then. Jess had left her fracturing parents behind, her face set towards London and the fairytale hope of happier endings. When Kate was a student, leaving South Africa was seen as a betrayal of the struggle. In the new democracy that tie has loosened. The new generation is set free, no need for loyalty.

I must put these thoughts behind me, cleave to my better self, she decides. Blow my nose, dry my eyes. Harness my mind, apply my thoughts exclusively to things that comfort and soothe.

The burglar alarm monitor winks its light at her as she moves towards the front door, but she never bothers to activate it. She hates the idea of surveillance, won't even have a cellphone in case it is a way she can be monitored. Her dogs, pushing ahead of her out of the house, are her protectors. Kate clumps outside, the screen door squealing and banging behind her. Please god that didn't wake Da, she worries. I cannot deal with him now. Today belongs to Storm and Sky; it belongs to the damaged future, not to the incompetent, incontinent present.

The hood of cloud has split open further; light has spilt through to fill the sky after the first tentative smudge. Gert has already loaded and secured the empty and sterilised urns into the back of the bakkie, so Kate climbs in and drives off, dogs bounding alongside. She greets his skraal figure over in the paddock with a wave of her hand.

No response.

So hard to know what is going on in the mind of another, one's own mind leaping frantically from one assumption to another, trying to make sense of the world. Each of us squatting in the small cloister of our brains, trying to decode meaning out of gesture and tone, clumsily attempting to decipher each other.

Gert has become a surly bugger, she broods. I am not in the mood for his moods.

She stops at the gate, brake on, the vehicle in neutral. Climbs out and has to lift the gate open – another maintenance job awaiting Gert's attention. Kate fights a frisson of irritation. She commands the dogs to stay, climbs back in and drives on, the wheels drilling briefly over the cow grid.

The road runs between green pastures, where farm workers are herding cows towards the milking sheds.

In front of her, to the north, is the berg, the raised and undulating terrain that gathers up random wanderings of the eye, directing attention to the drama of ascents and plateaus, rocks and earth caught up in the story of the continent's process, one that rests briefly for centuries as though meditating before shifting on and over the knife-edge of the present.

The mountain range stands and surveys the distant sea across this coastal stretch of land that humans have scratched at for a few hundred years, extracting a living.

Kate loves this land, has loved it ever since she was a child and Da bought the farm and left his banking life behind.

Unwittingly, she has followed in her father's footsteps, rejecting city life for the country. She wonders whether it is possible to live a life of one's own, one that is not either aligned towards or away from one's parents' choices. Which were, in their time, aligned towards or away from their parents?

The baton is handed down to the next generation, the story repeats itself, spiralling down the long twist of time and chromosomes.

Her bedroom is still the one from her childhood,

for heaven's sake. She is now doing her mother's job of looking after her father.

She slows to avoid a large puddle – a sheen of slate grey in the dark mud. Last winter, the rains further degraded the road, as does Wilhelm's practice of using a public thoroughfare to herd his cows from pasture to pasture instead of sorting out gates within his own property. Kate resolves to bring this up again at the next co-op meeting, although no one other than her friend and neighbour Daniel takes a female farmer seriously. Nor her mode of cheese making. She is seen as quaint, mad, old-fashioned. Luddite.

During the recent and increasingly frequent power cuts, Kate smirked back at her neighbours. She carried on milking while they argued about the cost of generators over herds of lowing and swollen cows. Kate's herd is milked by hand, the old way, before Edison and Eskom brought goodness and light and modernity to humankind. She prefers candlelight and gas with solar power as backup. Anarchist, she has always loved blackouts, as long ago as boarding school. Back then, it signified a loss of control of those in authority. Candlelight lapping gently away at the edges of darkness was a victory for those who felt powerless. Power cuts, nowadays, feel like an antidote for avaricious and wasteful ways.

The corrugations irritate. The local farmers do not share her concern that transporting fresh milk over ruts and potholes can break it and begin a butter-making process, thereby affecting the quality of the cheese. With their huge trucks and four-by-four vehicles and their embracing of mechanised processes, a few ruts in the road are very low on the agenda. The local farmers gather in the warm camaraderie of the Valley Hotel pub, drinking and swapping anecdotes and tips, and laughing, most probably at her. Those who appreciate what she does, no, more than that, those who believe in what she does, allow her to survive this peasant existence. The top chefs and the up-market delis order what was once ubiquitous and is now a rarity – cheese made with whole unpasteurised milk, hand-made in the old tradition, cheese with a taste and texture that is an experience, a delight, a delicacy.

Most people mistake the mass-produced, yellow blocks of plastic in supermarkets for cheese. Oom Gert explained to her as a child why Cheddar and Gouda are dyed yellow: The best, richest milk in spring yields cheese that is a deeper yellow than summer produce.

He also told her that commercial Cheddar is wrapped in a black plastic covering to emulate the real thing. A truckle of natural Cheddar grows a fungus on the surface, which is rubbed regularly into the cheese, forming a black rind.

That's why she forgives him his daily trespasses, old Gert. He helped her to see what is wrong with the world. The lies and veneer that have become the foundation of our civilised culture.

Crippling grief, threatening. Kate keeps her foot on the accelerator, her hands on the wheel. She glances at her watch. Five thirty-two. Three thirty-two in London. The tide of time, pushing us all forward.

Pull yourself together, Kate! Da's refrain from her childhood. Only now does she understand his point of view. She reprimands herself: I have things to do. I cannot be waylaid by this.

Focus on what is in front of you, she commands her will. Do the next thing, and the next. The next. Life as a long, cobbled chain of next things, providing a feeble filament of sorts to hold on to, to pull yourself through.

Kate turns left onto the national highway for the brief stretch before she reaches the gravel road on the right that leads to Harry's farm and the berg. There is unusually little traffic. Enormous yellow vehicles are standing around in the scrapes of the ongoing road works, leaning on their appendages, awaiting the arrival of their drivers. For months their metal teeth have been eating into the fragile reserve either side of the tar.

This development is surely not extreme enough to make Kate want to pull the bakkie over, leap out with her penknife, and stab, stab, *stab*, viciously, until she penetrates those massive grader tyres. But rage ignites the will, it gathers up slack and tired muscle. Kate is awake now, her hands clench the wheel; she is ready to kill.

Always creating a drama. Da's voice, poking fun at her. Over-reacting again. Look, she's going for an Oscar, he'd hoot. Binding Kate's protest with his ridicule.

A flock of bright yellow bishop birds rises from the verge, swirling. Making do with the few remains of habitat humans have unintentionally left them in the space between the road and the fields. What will you do, where will you go, sweet creatures, she anguishes, when we humans have taken everything?

Yet Kate, too, is complicit. She can list many of

the must-haves she is immune to, but a vehicle, for example, would not be on it; without this old bakkie, she knows she could not do trade in cheese. Real mozzarella in particular, which must be eaten within three days of the making.

Kate used to think she could not do without a piano. Hah! she snorts. For ever so long it has had to do without her.

In front of Harry's milking shed is a spanking new bakkie, lifted straight out of an advert for agricultural success. Kate catches herself gazing at it with longing. Harry's dairy farm is large and fully mechanised, and his yield is up to thirty thousand litres of milk a day.

Harry is nowhere to be seen. The cows just milked are pushing out of the large shed through one door, while others with turgid udders enter from the far end, where farm workers are hustling them into place. One young man is shouting at a recalcitrant cow and striking her with a hose, encouraging her to turn around as she is facing the wrong way in the milking stall. She pulls her head this way and that to evade the sting, bellowing, yet refuses to turn; stubborn or obtuse, it is hard to say.

The fate of the milk cow: lifelong wet-nurses for

humans, their own young removed in order to keep human babies alive and thriving. Kate remembers her astonishment when she learnt that humans are the only animals that drink milk into adulthood.

I suckled you at my own breast, she points out to her distant daughter. You had a human for a mother, not a cow. You flourished on my own sweet milk.

Jess gave up breastfeeding the twins early on. The configuration of their conjoined heads was too difficult for her to hold while nursing.

Kate reverses up to one of the stainless steel milk storage tanks and gets out of her bakkie. She unties the rope and aims the nozzle of the large diameter hose into the first urn and opens the valve. Fresh, steaming white liquid pulses out, then gushes.

It takes only a few minutes and all five urns are full.

Five times forty litres is two hundred litres of cow's milk, which will convert over the next three months into a twenty-kilogram truckle of Cheddar. Two simple yet complex twists provide a miracle: grass into milk, milk into cheese. The ancient, essential process of preserving milk.

If she goes to England, there will be no one to fetch the cow's milk. If she is away for one week, her

Cheddar cheese production alone drops by over one hundred and forty kilograms of cheese.

Daniel, the Jewish pig farmer down the road who thinks he's in love with her, is always quick to offer help. But he has his own workload to attend to, and she does not have much to give him in return for his kindnesses.

Two minutes past six. Four a.m. in London. She should speak to Sharon first, before phoning Jess. Kate climbs into the cab and starts up the engine.

She drives back slowly, avoiding puddles and potholes in a road flanked by wet fields. Past Harry's hill of silage under plastic sheeting held down by old tyres – fodder fermenting, stored for the summer, when the pastures are poor. Cheese only tastes as good as what you put into it, Missie Kate, Gert taught her. She knows now, from experience: The quality of the elements and the ingredients – water and minerals, proteins and sunlight, carbohydrates and the condition of the soil and the lactating animal – all these factors determine the quality of the end product.

She remembers a lovely quote: 'In order to make an apple pie from scratch, you must first create the universe.' To think: the whole universe, concentrated in this gift of milk. There are moments when Kate understands this mystery, and her spirit lifts.

Here comes Tractor Sam, cap on, along the road, manoeuvring with his severed steering wheel. Kate slows down. Poor kid, she thinks. Or perhaps not. Perhaps he is content with his lot. He believes there is a tractor attached, and loves nothing better than to drive it out of his parents' yard, and into the world, his feet wheeling. He carefully manipulates his imaginary vehicle, his mouth and lips making engine sounds as he negotiates the corrugated gravel with his bare feet, hooting vehemently whenever he sees another vehicle approaching. Toot! Toot! – his lips below his moustache funnel the warning.

Kate waves as she passes, and he responds with a gap-toothed grin, too careful a driver to risk releasing a greeting hand off the steering wheel. In his twenties, at a guess. They say he was born strange, and stayed that way.

He recedes in her rear-view mirror, a small character who occupies the entire landscape.

As far as Kate is aware, he has never had an accident.

The sky is clotted with cloud, but the background blue is clear, rinsed by the night's rain. The farmer's need to know the weather blurs with Kate's artistic appreciation of cloudscapes – the infinite variety of forms: misty wisps and erupted whites above the underlining of the land.

Kate's small farm appears over the rise, nestled in beside the dam – an oasis of fynbos and indigenous trees that stand out in a vast green desert of pastures and fields. It does feel like home, she thinks. Yet I am an interloper, always.

Across the water lies the stretch of fields that her father subdivided and sold three years ago. Kate suspects that this was the first sign of his decline. Or an overreaction to her mother's death. It did not occur to him to speak to his three daughters about this nor any other decision. He was not able to see her love of this land, tied as it was with her love of him and his break from a desk-trapped life. That old cluster of rage, regret and recrimination congregates beneath Kate's diaphragm.

Her father had dismissed Kate's objections, saying

that farming was not the life for a girl. When she objected further, a weird smile crept onto his face, and he pointed out, with an aggrieved yet oddly triumphant air, that Beth was married to a city-bound manufacturer of chip flavourants, Pippa's boyfriend was an airhead, and Kate was divorced. Emphasising his point that only men would do. She decided right then that she would come here and show him. Now her father is too far gone to appreciate what she has achieved.

You do like playing the martyr, was Beth's contribution to Kate's decision, as she held her teacup in front of her like a shield. And it's far too late for playing happy families.

Beth was displaying their mother's diamond engagement ring on her finger. Kate was shocked to find that her mother had bequeathed all her jewellery to Beth when she died; not that she ever wears rings, but Kate is still hungry, hungry for her mother.

There's Da, in his frayed and battered panama hat, striding towards the hen coop in his long cadaverous frame, the short figure of Elihle shadowing him. As his daughter drives up to the house, Da sees the bakkie and veers back towards her. Kate can see before she hears that he is shouting.

Kate cuts the engine. Her father is right beside the bakkie, grabbing the sill of the open window with both hands and leaning in. Where is she? he asks, breathing old breath into her face. His features are torn open with anxiety, his eyebrows riding high.

Mind, Da. Kate says, slowly opens the driver's door, manoeuvring him backwards, careful not to scrape his shins with their paper-thin skin. She levers herself out.

Where has she gone? he wants to know, hunching his shoulders and showing her the large, hopeless palms of his hands.

Kate feels sorry for him, but she cannot touch him. She is unable to take his hands in hers, and cradle them, as a daughter should. She's gone to town, Da, she tells him. She'll be back later.

Oh, he says, nodding. Town. He sinks his hands into his pockets, stares over his daughter's shoulder a moment, then wanders off, mumbling and fiddling with something in the slack of his trouser leg. Da's pockets are always full of things he picks up. She has cautioned Elihle to monitor what her father collects after Nosisi found dry dog turd in a trouser pocket in the washing basket. She nods a greeting at the youngster, who is an absolute blessing, but whose days here must surely be numbered. No one can put up with this for long.

There will be a brief respite now, until Da again starts looking for his wife, forgetting that she is permanently in town. Town has become a metaphor for the afterlife; it is an explanation for everything. Not that Kate's mother had ever been interested in shopping. She was far happier in her veggie garden than in a supermarket or a boutique. Yet somehow, Da does not argue with this unlikely explanation.

If only Mum had not fallen ill, Da would not have needed the money to pay for her chemo and medication – the unbelievable price of hope in the modern age. If she hadn't died, he wouldn't have sold off the land on the other side of the dam. He wouldn't have lost his mind.

His wife had been his anchor, his attachment to place and time and meaning. Without her, he drifts through the days, anxious, puzzled, raging.

Losing Mum, we lost everything, Kate declares.

What nonsense! she corrects herself. Incredible how the mind veers persistently towards sentiment, like a faulty rudder.

Into the house, to fetch the bottle of starter culture from the oven where it has been incubating overnight. Back to the bakkie, where she clambers into the driver's seat, wedging the bottle between her thighs, then drives over to the cheese room and reverses up to the door.

Sharon is the one she wants to phone.

Gert is walking over from the goat hok with his ambling stride, wiping his hands on his pants, his face concentrated around some thought. He takes a hand-rolled smoke out of his shirt pocket and lights up; his head is wreathed in the grey exhalation of smoke for a moment before it fades in the air. Breath made visible. Then he coughs up a globule of phlegm and spits it into a bush. Frustration mixed with nausea runs through Kate.

Turning away, she concentrates on untying the rope. Môre, she hears his greeting, through his sparse and knotted grey beard.

Kate struggles to adopt a reasonable tone. It's not good to spit, Oom Gert. You know that, she snaps, glancing in his direction. He shrugs, his shoulders riding an incorrigible wave. He will not comply, leaving her floundering in the void between logic and personality. It makes her want to get her old microscope out of its red felt-lined box and show him, forcing his antiquated viewpoint through the aperture of the lens and into the modern biological world: See there! Those are the germs you spread when you spit. You put us all in danger.

This is an aspect of the low grade warfare between them, a germ warfare.

Gert widens his mouth in a ragged smile, and says: What doesn't kill you makes you strong, Missie Kate.

The local clinic has cleared him of TB, attributing his chest problems to heavy smoking. But Kate decides to retest the herd this week. If Gert contracts *Mycobacterium bovis* from his own goats or his friends' and then infects her herd, that would mean her darlings and her income would be gone.

Gert stubs out his cigarette on the side of the steps, and tucks the remainder behind his ear. He has come to help Kate shift the urns of cow's milk out of the bakkie and over into the cheese room, then empty them into the stainless steel vat, centred in the cool, white-tiled space. Kate used to be able to move them herself, and took some pride in that, but nowadays they feel heavier to her, and her left shoulder complains.

Gert is older than she is, but his strung and wired body seems manufactured for physical work. Yet one day, they'll both be too old to lift these urns.

She takes the hose that runs from the taps, inserts the end into the cavity walls of the vat, and turns on the hot tap, while Gert positions a plank between the bakkie and the door. The two of them shift and slide the urns one by one out of the bakkie along the plank and into the cheese room, and up-end their contents into the vat. The pale mother liquid pours in, swirling and frothing. Still steaming from the blood heat of the innards of cows, a heat that will help incubate the lactose fermenters in the culture. Kate inoculates the milk with *Streptococcus lactis* and *Streptococcus cremoris*, mother's little helpers, she thinks of them, humming the Rolling Stones' song, although she knows it's the wrong analogy. These organisms participate in the forming and flavouring of the cheese. It is a great irony, she thinks, that in this modern age of regulation and technology none of the world's greatest cheeses would have been permitted to be cultured due to concerns about germs and adequate pasteurisation.

Kate, whose majors were in genetics and microbiology, has always loved the invisible world, teeming with many organisms that assist and enhance human lives.

Gert washes his hands, then squirts a shot of pure alcohol onto them and gives them a good rub, grudgingly conceding his employer's point that there is a place for sterility in cheese making, and besides the danger of tuberculosis, there are other organisms that taint rather than enhance the final product. He flicks his hands to dry them, then sticks a finger into the milk and stands for a moment with the faraway look of a farmer testing the direction of the wind.

Amper daar, Missie Kate, he declares. Although he is usually remarkably accurate, and can differentiate thirty degrees from twenty eight, Kate pops the thermometer into the tank, where it bobs like a buoy in a white sea. This annoys Gert, but his employer is again underlining that in the ancient craft of cheese making there is a place for modernity.

The column of mercury reads twenty-eight.

In half an hour, Kate notes, she must add the rennet.

Gert ambles off to the goat hok to finish milking, and Kate goes across the field to the house to fetch yesterday evening's harvest of goat milk.

The path is a line of hard brown soil worn into and

through the grass by her own feet during the three years she has lived here. She thinks of it as the path of her pilgrimage, simultaneously back in time and towards her future. Some days, she regrets not building the cheese room closer to the house; on others, she loves the reassurance of the repeated stretch, part of the ritual of cheese. This rope of earth that connects work and home, holding her life together.

Passing the shed, Kate feels a subtle restraint against her thigh and stops quickly, but too late. She reverses as slowly as possible so as not to destroy the web entirely, but she has done too much damage. The substance that has the tensile strength to stop a bee in full flight has not survived her. The exquisite black and white striped spider comes hurrying along, hoping for a mammoth breakfast. Kate winds the remaining tangled strands around a post and resumes walking towards the kitchen.

Like us humans, the spider will have to start all over again, she broods. Like most of us, she will probably repeat her error.

The clock on the kitchen wall points its hands at six minutes to seven. Jess told her mother that the twins are going to theatre at seven GMT, that's in two hours' time. They will wake crying with hunger, kept fasting for their ordeal. The surgery will take all day, the tender severing of heads where they are joined awry at the crown. She imagines their tiny hands reaching towards and touching each other's faces, perhaps for the last time.

Only nine litres' yield from yesterday evening, Kate estimates. I must sell off those goats that do not produce much milk. She says this often, but does nothing. Her heart is too soft towards those animals who have served her well. Bad business sense, she castigates herself. She paralyses her intention with arguments: The Ayurvedic approach to nourishment recommends that we eat nothing that has not been prepared with love. Preparation of food starts here, with the feeding and milking of goats.

In a starving world, love is a luxury. The poor can only afford cheap machine-produced cheese that has the texture and taste of plastic.

She lugs the pails over to the cheese room, where Gert has left the steaming container of this morning's yield, and is pleased to note that it has increased to around eleven litres. Combining the quantities into one container, she stirs in the culture, mould and a portion of the rennet. The remainder of the rennet goes into the cow's milk vat. Check – the temperature is right.

Time to set out the pyramid moulds.

Cheese came to me in a dream, Kate recalls. When she told Sharon, her friend exclaimed, Kate! You can't make a decision based on a dream! Good god, last night I dreamt I was going to have another baby. Sharon stuck a hand on her hip: Well, I don't think so.

Sharon had the snip, as she calls it.

In the cheese dream, Kate was looking for a lost goat, blundering through dense vegetation. She came upon a mansion overlooking the sea. Inside the huge reception room were tables laden with every kind of cheese imaginable – wedged and veined, encrusted with chalky white casings or hard waxy skins; crumbly, creamy, runny and firm. An old woman approached Kate and encouraged her to help herself. They were made with you in mind, she smiled. Unbuttoning her blouse, she released a breast and offered it to Kate. The old woman's nipple filled Kate's mouth with suck. The relief she felt on waking could not be ignored.

Kate did not mention the dream in her letter of resignation to Geoff. She told him that her father was ill and needed taking care of, also that she required time to pursue her music. He called her into his office, picked up her letter, tore it up and threw it into the bin. He thought he had divined the real reason.

Get over this idea that life in a culture is sentient, he began to lecture. We stand on the brink of a radical new therapy, as radical as antibiotics, or radiation, even anaesthetics in its time. There were people who wanted to ban printing presses when they were first invented. People still object to nuclear power, even though it's been proven to be the most efficient and eco-friendly option. Progress requires a review, you have to interrogate your assumptions. For Chrissakes, Kate, you're one of my best embryologists. If we get this right for the funders, we could make a packet *and* improve the wellbeing of mankind. Not to mention the kudos if our lab beats the others in the race. Those are worthwhile goals, ones that rarely come round in a lifetime.

Geoff stared at his employee, not believing that he was not getting through. Then he went for the low swipe. Go then, he said coldly, leaning back and folding his arms. It is not as though you are irreplaceable. Most embryologists would give their eye teeth to be in on this project.

He turned to his monitor and started typing away, indicating that he no longer considered Kate to be in the room, and aimed the last kick as though ruminating to himself: I only want serious scientists in this lab.

Geoff had been her mentor. He'd made her his personal project and assigned her to oversee major aspects of his ground-breaking research, including her name in journal articles.

Three years later, Kate tries to define the terror in her belly. How to weigh up whether one has made the wrong choices.

Stir the goat's milk slurry. Seven forty-four. Time for another cuppa.

The spider has not repeated her mistake, and is busy weaving connections on the same side of the path, from the pole to a daisy bush with its startled yellow flowers held open to the sun. This could be a sign, thinks Kate. The world speaks a different language.

A tiny shifting shadow on the verge stops her; it's a dung beetle manoeuvring a ball three times her size by standing on her front legs and pushing with her rear ones. Kate crouches to observe her brave effort as she struggles along, sometimes misjudging the timing and terrain and ending up on top of the dung ball, or slipping off to the side. Recovering her stance, pushing on.

Jou bliksem! Gert is shouting and waving his arms as he chases monkeys away from the hen coop; they are so quick to drop from the trees to steal eggs. For some inexplicable reason he insists on opening the coop before Nosisi arrives at eight, even though it's her job to collect the eggs before the monkeys do. The eternal war for the possession of eggs is waged around the hapless, squawking parent hen.

Leaving Gert to deal with it, Kate heads back to the house. The telephone has begun to ring, so she breaks into a run. Jess might have decided she needs her mother after all.

Hullo Doll! Only Sharon can get away with calling Kate 'Doll'. Sorry I missed your call last night. You'll never guess why. You heard from Jess?

No. They go to theatre in just over an hour.

Well, they can't go on like this, she says.

Sharon is one of the few people who has seen the photographs – the twins at two months old, on their backs, Storm gurgling up at the camera and kicking his legs, Sky more contemplative, with a fist in his mouth. Each arising out of the other's head like the parody of a thought bubble. Also the photos at eight months, showing their astonishing locomotive ability, working out how to lever themselves over together and crawl like an eight-legged spider, reading each other's minds about how to direct their efforts. Storm the more dominant, Sky the compliant, each co-ordinating their movements as one whole being.

Eighty percent chance Sky will die, Kate tells her friend, even if he survives he'll probably have a permanent disability. Storm's risks, they're less, but still awful.

Statistics are bloody unhelpful. Have you decided?

Pointless, seeing she doesn't want me there.

It's that god-bunch she's got in with.

They've warned her against her lost mother.

It's their Christian duty to forgive you.

Maybe I'm unforgiveable.

Kate searches through the kitchen drawers for a

tissue, serviette, anything, then gives up and wipes her eyes and nose on her shirt sleeve.

Oh Kate, we're all struggling along, doing the best we can.

There is a line of black, trickling up and down the wall in front of her. The ants have found the sugar bowl again. Ant queens don't have to deliberate about their offspring, she muses. Their young hatch and fall into line. None of this fretting and looping about whether you have done a good enough job.

Kate? You still there?

There's this whole roster of church women coming round to help with the babies. My presence would make things worse rather than better. Jess accuses me of being bossy, insensitive. Am I insensitive? she asks.

The time she visited, it hadn't ended well. Both of them were relieved when Kate caught her flight home.

You can be, um, a bit of a nag. I mean, I've heard you go on. At Jess. A bit.

You're one to talk. Look at you and Josh.

Josh! That's why I missed your call. I was under his bedroom window late last night. Down on my knees, pretending to weed the flower bed. Sniffing the air, trying to detect a waft of weed. It's pathetic.

I felt like a dog.

Sharon, we also smoked weed at that age, Kate reminds her. Lots of it.

She is fond of Joshua, a charming, disarming child who has metamorphosed into an inarticulate and angular adolescent.

I know, but we didn't have a *problem*.

Of course we did. Do. We still have problems.

How do I know he's not addicted? His grades are down, he's rude, won't talk –

Kate sighs. Today she doesn't know anything. If only we could tie our children to their beds where they'll be safe forever, she offers.

Nobody warned me they'd end up having minds of their own. I'm going to sew a condom onto his dick. Or arrange a marriage with the nice girl next door who loves me and will never, ever hate me.

Kate has to laugh: It is a bloody tightrope. Her voice wobbles.

Jeez, look at the time, and Josh's still not out of bed. Gotto go Doll. Chin up, I'll phone later.

Kate puts the kettle on. Leans against the counter, her arms folded over the pressure in her chest. Waiting for the curd to firm. Waiting for the phone to ring.

Waiting for a solution, an outcome, an ending.

A scrape of feet at the kitchen door and Nosisi enters, a new red scarf wrapped around her head.

Molo, her helper greets. She is surprisingly ebullient this morning.

That's pretty!

Nosisi touches her doek and smiles with pleasure: It's from Ntombi. She takes her apron off the hook behind the door and slips the loop over her head, proclaiming: Today will be good.

Well, we don't know that yet.

I saw iicelo, she explains. Right in my house.

Iicelo?

Those birds with the tail, what do you call them in English? The tail that goes like so – and she flattens her hand and tips it up and down at the wrist in a jerky movement.

Wagtails?

Ah, yes. Wagtails, two of them, come to feed on crumbs fallen from my table. It's a sign. The ancestors have come, answering my prayers.

That's what mothers do, Kate thinks, we put out bread, grasp at straws. To Nosisi she says: Luzoko will be fine, that's good.

Kate wishes she believed in signs, the natural world come to tell her that all will be well. Yesterday she saw a small green snake slithering across the driveway, a grass snake, so she didn't have to worry about the dogs. She did not tell Nosisi, who is terrified of snakes, harbingers of bad luck in her culture. Perhaps the bad luck was meant for Kate. Nosisi has heard the catch in Kate's voice, and looks at her sharply. You white people, she says, you don't know your ancestors. Those birds, on my birthday, they are a very good sign.

Oh my god. It is Nosisi's birthday, remembers Kate. Her brain is developing holes like ageing Swiss cheese. Information and arrangements falling through.

I have a gift for you, Kate lies, scrabbling about in her mind for an appropriate present. There is no such thing as popping out to the shop in this part of the world. Money is so impersonal, but it will have to do. She goes to the office and takes a hundred rand out of the safe.

That is too little, she hesitates. I owe this woman so much. Another hundred is not going to make a difference to my problems.

She adds another note, locks up, and goes through to the kitchen.

Nosisi, with a mildly irritated air, is sweeping up the mud that her employer's haste brought in earlier. Kate ignores this and opens her arms to the woman who came to work for her parents when she was only an adolescent. Kate takes her large body in her arms and holds it to hers, Nosisi's huge breasts squashing against her chest. There's a necklace of wrinkles lacing Nosisi's throat. They are both getting old.

Happy birthday. Kate offers the cash, regretting her carelessness in not putting it into an envelope with a card. Nosisi claps her hands, then cups them to receive the notes.

Enkosi! Her gratitude shames Kate who now regrets not giving her three hundred.

Have you heard from Luzoko? Nosisi shakes her head. Perhaps you will today, on your birthday.

She measures oats into the pot, saying: It is not allowed.

Nosisi adds water and fresh cow's milk from the fridge. Raisins, cinnamon and salt.

Luzoko was sickly as a baby, but both women know that even healthy young men can die of septicaemia during or after initiation in the bush. Ritual circumcision is a trial of manhood, one that can end in death.

Only those who are fit to be men will come through the ordeal. Only if an initiate survives without the comfort and help of the mother can he leave the arena of childhood.

There is enough suffering in the world without creating more, Kate once challenged Nosisi. She was surprised to hear the anger in her voice, knowing that Nosisi has no influence over this male ritual. The woman who works for her must take comfort in a sign from her ancestors. Whereas Kate has nothing to allay her fear but the science of the sterile scalpel.

She doesn't know whether the knife that cut Luzoko was a sterile one. Its purpose is to sever the son from the mother with the removal of the foreskin, which is seen as the skirt that covers the male genitals. Breaking with milk and warmth, exposing young manhood to pain, blood and the threat of death.

Perhaps it is necessary.

Nosisi takes a wooden spoon and stirs the porridge. She has already lost one child to meningitis. She is in need of signs. Perhaps you also don't need to worry today, she says, glancing at Kate.

Kate's ancestors a few generations back were soldiers, gold prospectors and drunks. They were train conductors and insecticide manufacturers, and ran boarding houses for the down-and-out. She cannot see any of them pitching up as birds to prophesy a good surgical outcome. But she's not going to argue the point.

The phone starts to ring. She hurries to answer, but it's Beth, her older sister.

I heard they're operating today.

Must be from Leonard. Kate is annoyed that her ex-husband informs her relatives. He is still regarded as family in her sister's house.

Waiting is the worst thing, Beth's voice assures. Remember when I thought Roy was on that plane that went down? That hour was one of the longest of my life, not knowing.

Right, Kate clips. I remember.

When are you going over? Beth asks, as though it's a walk to the cheese room. I thought you'd be there already. She herself is fresh back from a trip to Florence and Venice.

As soon as possible, Kate hears herself say. When things settle down.

They work miracles nowadays, you know. Did you see that programme where they showed a brain operation live on TV? They cured someone of Parkinson's so bad he was bedridden.

I don't have TV, she says. Beth still can't believe this.

A silence. Beth's bright telephone voice, trying again: Oh, did Margaret tell you? Jenny has been accepted to York University to do her master's. On a scholarship that covers everything.

Kate feels a crumpling: Her sister has taken a baton to the back of her knees.

Congratulations! Kates forces. You must be pleased with your brilliant daughter.

She sits, her legs incapable of holding her up. And Beth's off – on and on about her wonderful children and their shimmering lives. Elizabeth, I can't talk right now, she interrupts. I have to cut the curd.

The cheese, always the cheese, her sister remarks with a sharpened little voice. Give us a ring later.

Sit a while, Kate. Reassemble your cells. String your body back together on the thread of your will. Kettle on, yoghurt and muesli. Stupid cow, she retaliates as she spoons her breakfast into her mouth. Beth's kids seem so normal, so well-balanced. Jason ascending the corporate world, groomed to take over the family business, Jenny climbing the academic ivory tower in

English lit. The veneer will cave in eventually, Kate consoles herself, inserting slow thought needles into the image Beth has created of a model family. One day, she'll stand and watch them burn.

Oh, Jess! she grieves, envy active like a rat. What happened? Parents send their young off into the world as their special representatives of success, but Kate has raised her daughter to be different, to stand up to an idea of normal and what is expected by society. She did not foresee that one day her daughter would stand up to her.

Nor the specific form it would take: Jess's turning away from achievement and towards her new-found religion, some minor charismatic church that believes that only they are right and everyone else, including Kate, is wrong.

Bloody bugger, Da exclaims as he comes up the path towards the back door.

He never used to use such language, but his illness has undone his restraints. Once, before Elihle came into Kate's life, she found Da wandering round the yard without pants on. Yet, despite the incoherence of his life, he arrives promptly at mealtimes and eats like a horse, food disappearing into his mouth, absorbed without trace into his long stringy limbs.

Ten minutes past eight and the curd is waiting. Kate cannot deal with Da right now. Leaving the last of the muesli, she dodges out through the front door so as to avoid her father.

And walks over to the cheese room, where the vat of white has solidified satisfyingly into a giant block of curd. Taking the horizontal wire frame, she aligns it with the edge and digs down, then slices the curd across with an easy movement. Using the vertical wire frame, she cuts the curd down its length and breadth. The firm mass slowly collapses into a morass of pieces swimming within the yellowish whey. Slowly, repeatedly, Kate disturbs the small cubes of curd with the stirrer. Her life is reduced every day to these small acts of waiting for something to complete itself. The rennet and the lactic acid, acting. Gently she stirs, lest the fragile curds disintegrate; slowly she moves the implement through, encouraging the whey to weep, to seep out of the curd. She has learnt, living this life, that some things cannot be hastened, some things are worth waiting for.

She wonders about neurosurgeons, whether operating on the brain must be done as fast as possible, or whether there is a considered and tempered rhythm.

In her previous life, she'd spent hours looking at potential human beings down microscopes, patiently fertilising, culturing, gently pipetting sperm cells and ova and embryonic cells, checking humidity and acidity and temperature levels. Life is only possible within a tiny margin of conditions. Her work not only encouraged reproduction in the childless but also the best possible outcome: the healthy, well-formed child, DNA-checked for defects, quality approved. Playing god, only much more carefully. Being more exact than nature, than nature's purported creator.

Geoff's funders wanted to take things a step further than Kate's conscience would allow. Their proposal troubles her still – using discarded embryos to investigate methods of generating human tissue for transplant. Incredible what we have discovered, she thinks, while stirring, still stirring: Insert a pluripotent human cell next to embryonic kidney tissue, and you can grow renal cells exactly like the original donor's. No problems with rejection. No side effects from rejection-suppressing drugs. Wreck your heart or pancreas or liver, and Cloning Inc. can grow you a new one. If you can afford it.

With tiny, cumulative steps, humans have crossed several thresholds – from aborting foetuses to creating embryos in the lab, to retaining some for making babies and disposing of the rest, to keeping the reject zygotes alive to experiment upon. It makes her sick with worry: That all the splendour and mystery of life on earth has been tethered and yoked in service of the human will.

So Kate changed from culturing embryos to culturing cheese. Few understood why she left the lab. Beth rolled her mascara-spiked eyes when she heard that her sister was giving up modern, groundbreaking work to become a technophobic farmer, as she put it.

If I fail, thinks Kate, and Beth is shown to be correct, I will consider the world doomed.

The curds have begun to firm. Kate puts the stirrer down, takes off her wristwatch and slips it into her pocket. She washes her hands and arms right up to above her elbow. Like a surgeon about to operate, she disinfects, rendering herself harmless, blameless. Inserting her arm up to the elbow, she runs her hand through the vat with open fingers, stopping to pinch the substance. Stirring to ensure that the increasingly weighty curd does not compact too soon onto the bottom of the vat. She pinches again, assessing it for the right moment to cease this disturbance, the moment she will allow the solid to precipitate. Slowly she performs this gesture, her back twinging at this angle. Ceasing a moment, she pulls her shoulders down and back to release the spasm.

Kate observes her hand, wet with whey. It is an implement, a willing servant, awaiting instruction born of thought. Everything around her – the shed, the hose, the cheese, the bakkie parked outside, the fence, the vegetable garden – all of it is evidence of human thought made word made substance. If we had the anatomy of dolphins or tortoises, she reflects, we could devise brilliant ideas but be unable to impact them onto our environment. Or it could be that the hand's multiple functions – extracting, constructing, developing, designing, creating, modifying and destroying – was a stimulus to develop the brain's capacity. She imagines neurons sprouting out new dendrites, new connections, fed by the activity of the miracle of the hand.

Bend again to the task: stirring.

She has read that there are more synapses in the human brain than there are stars in the Milky Way. The grey mushroom housed in the skull, not much larger than two fists, must have limits on how accurately it can think about itself. Like trying to cut into a chainsaw using the same chainsaw. How can something that has arrived by random chance, or intelligent design, or any other mechanism, even begin to contemplate itself and come up with the right answers?

Sharon, one happily drunken night, postulated that the entire universe is a molecule in the right thigh of a god who laughs uproariously at the theories humans come up with to explain reality.

The curd is still too soft. Kate's back is aching but she must continue her solitary shift.

Leonard's voice, accusing Kate over the phone: Why have you isolated yourself? What are you running away from?

At first she had taken his question seriously, unable to respond. Once she had put the phone down, she wished she'd said: I wanted to distance myself from all the people determined to report your latest sexual escapades to me. Three years on, she is past caring who he inserts his neediness into.

The clots of milk are resisting her pressure and

keeping their shape. The consistency is about right.

Gert taught her this craft, passing on his skill and experience from years of keeping his own goats. He showed Kate so that she can save what is left of the farm and also save herself. That is how she thinks of it.

Gert comes in from cleaning down the goat hok, picks up the milk pail and pours the slurry into the moulds. He watches the trickle of whey collect and leak from the tray as the moulds drain. Springertjie has an infected teat, he informs his employer. He is pleased when an animal has to have antibiotics, for then the milk cannot be used for cheese that is marketed as 'organic', and Gert can take the produce for his own use. He shakes his head at the thought that the rich are so fussy. The poor can't afford to throw anything away except their own phlegm.

Kate will have to see to the little doe who is one of her favourites, despite not being a great producer. She has a sweet nature and stands still for the milking, unlike Duiweltjie who you have to watch in case she kicks the pail, which she does on purpose, splashing a morning's produce onto the muddy, straw-strewn floor. No use crying over it, as they say.

Gaan eet as jy klaar is, Kate tells him.

Gert steps outside and clamps a butt between his lips. He lights a match, scrape and flare, cupping his hands around the flame and leaning towards it to ignite the tip, inhaling. He turns in the direction of the house. Through the window Kate watches him as he walks towards breakfast.

The curd between the tips of her fingers feels like pieces of brain.

Disgusting how my own brain ambushes me, Kate thinks with the self-same organ. There is a painful tightening in her throat.

It should be possible to operate on one's thoughts. To excise the tendency to think back on regrettable incidents. To cauterise guilt. Or ablate desire for repeatedly being attracted to the wrong kind of person. Operations and injuries to the brain can alter personality, she knows this. They can increase docility or aggravate aggression. She worries whether her grandsons will retain their personalities. She will never know what they would have been like if …

A terrible word: 'if'. Conjoined as it is to the word 'only'.

If only all this would go away, she wishes. I wish to cut these feelings out, these situations that should never happen to anyone. I wish to excise and incinerate my upset and get on with my life.

Eight forty-three here, six forty-three there. No stopping the inevitable. The surgeons and the anaesthetist have entered the theatre changing room; they are unlacing and kicking off their shoes. What do they talk about while they remove their street clothes and hang them up, then slip on green garments, tying caps on, masks over mouths and noses? Surely, they must be nervous as they insert their feet into white boots, then push the theatre doors open. She wonders whether they sweat, whether their hands shake.

The twin's condition is so rare; the neurosurgeons could not have had much opportunity to practice this operation.

Soon the babies will be taken away from Jessica and wheeled into theatre in their cot, their small linked bodies a mirror reflection of each other at the interface of their skulls.

Jess will feel it in her belly – the tearing.

The masks will descend over their faces, an intravenous line will be inserted; but they will need more than one. They share the same blood system, connected through their scalps and brains. But there will be an afterwards when one is divided into two, when her grandsons are untied and their lives can suddenly and completely go off in different directions.

After the shock of the ultrasound that revealed the twins' condition, Daniel found the story on the internet of the original conjoined male twins – Siamese twins, born in Siam in another age – who were attached at the waist. Their parents sold them off when they were children to a manager from America who was looking for spectacles for his sideshow circuit. They travelled the world for most of their lives, earning a good living from people's desire to ogle the grotesque.

Child abuse, we would call that now, she thinks. Nowadays, we diagnose conjoined twins *in utero* with the aid of ultrasound and abort the problematic ones, rather than allow them a bizarre and difficult life; or, as in Jessica's case, if the mother will not agree to an abortion, we separate them after birth at risk of death.

Those Siam twins lived their whole lives together, marrying twin sisters and having twenty-one children between them. Kate contemplates what it would be like to have Beth breathing down her neck and making snarky comments every time she made love to her husband. Or if Leonard's priest brother had to be dragged along to every seduction ...

Sharon had also supplied Kate with stories garnered from the internet, telling her about conjoined female twins who had lived into their fifties joined at the crown in such a way that they looked in different directions. They lived together in an apartment, a four-legged creature. One was a gospel singer while the other played guitar. Together they won awards. They only ever saw each other's faces by the use of several mirrors and had different personalities despite sharing major brain structures.

Joined the way they are, Kate had felt overwhelmed by the enormity of the problem, even as the twins drank and slept and defecated, unconcerned by their deformity. Looking at them, innocent, beautiful – also a two-bodied monster – Kate kept wanting to weep. Her hands were restless, empty. At night, on the sleeper couch in her daughter's awful, cold flat, Kate was filled with the desire to suck her thumb, an old boarding-school comfort. Suck, suck, trying for sustenance. The next morning she went down to the local deli and came back laden with food, which she cooked and baked and ate. She was trying to help in her own way, but it went unappreciated. Jess exploded and told her to go home. Kate still aches to think of it, the confusion of not understanding exactly what it was that she had done wrong. She had filled up Jess's freezer and flew back to her round of goats and cheese.

Jessica has barely spoken to Kate since. Prefers council social workers and women's church groups to her own mother.

Kate checks the position of the sieve at the outlet, then opens the tap at the bottom of the vat, allowing the whey to follow gravity down a hose and into the barrel outside. Food for Daniel's livestock.

Leaving the curd to settle and compact, she walks back to the house. The surface of the dam is very still today despite clouds drifting and shredding above, patching the land with wandering shade. Her feet are heavy with dread.

Gert is sitting on a bench on the back stoep eating his porridge. He will not eat in the kitchen, even when it is cold or raining. In this respect, he cannot shrug off the dictates of the old days when kleurlinge sat on the back of the bakkie and outside the back door. Or maybe it has more to do with Nosisi keeping him out of her domain. The interminable butt is lodged behind his ear.

Gooi jou sigarette weg, Gert. Dit gaan jou siek maak, slips out, despite the pointlessness of the remark. He shrugs. Gert has only one shrug but somehow manages to convey a host of meanings. She stamps inside, ostensibly to knock off clods. Perhaps she is a nag, after all.

Kate remembers that she wants to raise the issue of the damp in the bathroom again, but his resistance feels exhausting.

Da and Elihle are busy with breakfast. Da won't allow anyone but his daughter to feed him. When he feeds himself, porridge ends up on the table, on his bib, and on the floor, where the dogs wait gratefully. Elihle attempts to help direct the food into Da's mouth which sometimes results in porridge landing on the young man.

While Da is creating a huge mess, Elihle is trying to clean it up – a dispiriting task. Kate has suggested he leaves the clearing up until after the meal. But the young man is so willing, so dedicated, that he engages at every opportunity. His own porridge grows cold.

Eat, Kate tells him, taking the sticky spoon out of her father's grasp. As she sits down on a chair opposite, he inserts his hand into his porridge and licks his fingers. She scoops up a mouthful and offers it. This is worse than having an infant, she despairs. Da's brain is growing increasingly infantile and dependent.

She wonders whether her father's fondness for alcohol was a factor, whether recurrent intoxication can result in a permanent form of inebriation without alcohol. Since moving to the farm she has locked the drinks cupboard, but Da doesn't seem to miss his regular tots, lost as he is in the fog of his current state.

Every time he leans forward and opens his mouth to receive the spoon, his eyebrows lift as though activated by the same string. Forward, open, up. Back, close, down. Chew. Swallow, his throat muscles working. Repeat.

That's it, Da, she encourages him.

One of the original male Siamese twins was an alcoholic, the other a teetotaller. When the drunk got drunk, they both did, and when he died of alcoholic complications, the other one followed before they had time to sever him. Some cuts can save a life. Sometimes being too close to someone can kill you.

Da has stopped eating and stares at his daughter, puzzled. What have you done to your hair, Mary? he asks.

Kate has given up pointing out to him that she is not his wife. I grew it, Kate tells him. Eat up, Da, your porridge is getting cold.

He opens his mouth obediently, using the surprise mechanism of his eyebrows, and she shovels in the last few spoonfuls.

At the sound of the back door opening, Da swivels in his seat to see Gert stepping into the kitchen and putting his bowl on the counter. He looks from Gert to Elihle to Nosisi, then leans towards Kate, staring conspiratorially over the red slack of his lower lids. You know, he warns grimly, the blacks are taking over.

Kate used to squirm. Now, she just grins wryly at Nosisi and agrees: Yes, Da, it's about time.

Gert takes the cup of coffee that Nosisi has grudgingly left for him on the counter and leaves, the screen door banging. Nosisi stares crossly out of the window at his retreating figure.

I don't want a repeat of yesterday, Kate decides, with Nosisi refusing to wash Gert's plate. It's pathetic, the way adults behave. Gert can be rude, but she must learn to ignore it. Kate suspects that she is asserting the superiority of the kitchen over the fields.

Elihle is wiping Da's mouth and hands with a warm wet cloth, gently separating his fingers to do an exact job. Kate likes this youngster, she was drawn to him from the first day Nosisi brought him to the farm. He'd dropped out of school to care for his sick parents until they died, one after the other, presumably of AIDS, and he was in need of employment.

He has a mild and well-proportioned face, full lips and perfect teeth. If he were taller and female, he could have been a model.

Thank you, Elihle, she acknowledges. He nods shyly. Hardly says a word.

Nine o'clock, so it's seven there. Kate takes the telephone and goes through to the sitting room, annoyed that privacy is so hard to come by in this house.

In the corner stands her mother's piano, a silent reminder. The instrument admonishes her like a neglected dog eyeing its master, willing her to go for a walk. I want to play the piano again, she told Geoff when handing in her resignation. I can't find the time in the city.

Her employer had stared at Kate in disbelief. On that point he turned out to be right. It wasn't city life that kept her from playing. Some restraint still binds her, or some faulty connection between desire and the long path down her arms to her fingertips. Also a hesitation of the heart, perhaps, that interferes with the shapes her hands are required to make – no, not only the hands, but her whole body – in order to lean into the music.

The chords that arrived in her mind that morning sound out again, striking the strung neurons in the grand piano of her brain. She shakes her head in despair. How to transfer that perfection, to allow the music formed within Mozart's mind and applied to paper to flow in through the apertures of her eyes, into and out of her brain, then to her fingertips, and into and then out of the piano, releasing great compositions into the world.

That afternoon, when the restaurant guests have gone, she will try again, laying her hands down upon the keys, and attempt to make some sense of her life.

The telephone handset weighs heavily in her hand; she positions her finger on the green button. Now, she tells herself, depress it. The earpiece emits a dialling tone, ready to receive her instructions to connect.

The framed photo of Jess on the piano catches her eye. Kate can recall taking the shot, where she was standing, and the tension she felt, watching her daughter that day. She is six, smiling gap-toothed and gleeful down at her mother from the apex of the arc of a swing at the park near where they lived. Her hands clutched tightly around the chains, causing them to angle. Jessica had very little fear, even after her fall from a tree the previous summer, whereas Kate always had to fight the nausea of her anxiety. Perhaps her daughter engaged in risky activities as a child, like running as fast as she could downhill, to see the alarm on her mother's face. Perhaps that is still the case.

Look at me! Jess says to her from the photo. Look what I can do! Through the eye of the camera, Kate took and pinned her accomplishment to paper. The best I could do, as a mother, she wants to explain, was to swallow my fear.

Jessica had no idea what lay in store for her, for us.

I was the goddess at the centre of her world, the ground of her being. In that photo I still am.

The earpiece whirrs a while and then stops dead. Kate cannot bring herself to activate the chain of numbers that will lead to her daughter. How to ask: Why would you not want your mother? Each word impaled onto the skewer of that sentence.

And she is sitting beside the ICU bed the day Jess fell from the tree, her daughter's scraped and swollen face far too small against the stark, hard hospital pillow. Unable to hold her. To do so she has to move her and any movement makes her semi-conscious child cry. Instead, she sings her favourite nursery rhyme, *Twinkle, Twinkle Little Star*, strokes her hand, and weeps. Her mother, Mary, arrives, takes one calculating look and turns away. Not much we can do here, she proclaims. I'm sure she'll be okay. Then leaves for the farm. Kate wants to rail at her mother, yet she swallows her words, knowing it is better that way. Her mother is no use to her.

Kate turns from the photo, away from Jessica. So glad her child survived, so sad it has come to this.

Nosisi is beside her, placing a steaming mug on the coffee table.

Thanks.

Oh Jessie, Nosisi shakes her head. May God by her side.

May Jess's mother be with her, Kate wants to correct. Instead, she says: I'm not sure that God has a vested interest in how this turns out.

Nosisi clicks her tongue. These things are too big for us to see. Only God can see. He will tell us what to do.

I'll keep my ears open, Kate sighs to herself, thinking: It must help to believe in a benevolent Father.

She takes the mug and goes to sit on the front stoep to be alone before it's time to start the Cheddaring.

A pair of witogies are ferreting about in the wild dagga bush that has seeded itself at the end of the stoep. Impossible to observe their bright, quick movements and remain enraged or despondent. Birds, she speculates, are the original antidepressant. It's no wonder that wagtails can be seen as representatives of good news.

She wonders how pleasure operates. How the surge of warmth and recognition is evoked when watching birds. Andy, her colleague at the lab, used to reduce everything to a molecular biological level. When Kate told him she was going farming, he quoted some research findings that gardeners and farmers are less depressed. Scientists think it is because bacteria in the earth release a precursor to serotonin, which people who tend to the soil inhale while working.

Kate is bemused at the idea that humans are merely organisms floating around in a primordial soup at the mercy of the ebb and flow of chemical compounds. A handful of soil from her vegetable garden is one of the things that helps her to reconcile dead remains with future life. Living close to the earth is a constant reminder of cycles and tides, and she finds this revitalising.

Yet now, in the age of drought, food insecurity, farm murders and cheap imports, she wonders whether the smell of soil and the sight of birds is enough to keep a farmer's spirits up.

The thick thrust of trees in front of the house draws her attention up to the sky. It is an inverted ocean today, a deep reservoir of startling blue, with long lines of clouds unravelling slowly towards the berg like repeating wave crests. A pair of swallows is flitting and diving at different tempos. Lento and allegro, co-existing. To the east, she is relieved to see a yellow-billed kite pulsing its way across the sky. There's a whole other world here, she consoles herself, one that puts our failed humanity into perspective.

Then she's leaping to her feet, shouting: You fuckers! Fuck off!

In the field on the other side of the dam, there are three small men with a tripod, gesticulating and pacing, writing on clipboards.

The men continue measuring and conferring. It is too far for them to hear her. Nosisi, however, comes hurrying out, and Da appears from around the corner of the house, his tortoise neck straining out of his collar, Elihle in tow.

Where? Where are they? her father shouts, one arm raised as though to ward off a blow, his movements tense and angular. He swings on Elihle. Leave me! he commands, his hands beating the air as though to shoo away a cloud of flies. Leave me alone, for Chrissakes!

Swivelling back, his eyes search Kate's face with apprehension. Mary, he confides, we really should go home now. They are following me. There is saliva glistening in the groove at the corner of his mouth; the skin of his neck is loosened into two long folds that attach his chin to the knobs of his collar bones.

Okay, Da, we'll be going home just now. She understands his paranoia. Those suited men have followed her here. Commerce is setting up shop right in front of her secluded haven. She wants to explain to her father that he is deluded in his pursuit for a home. There is no safe place to escape.

First I have to turn the cheese, she tells him. Sit down so long. Don't be in such a hurry. You were always in such a hurry.

Oh, he says, as though this is a new thought. He sits on the bench abruptly, as if a puppeteer had suddenly lost interest.

His eyes wander up to Elihle's face, staring at him without comprehension. Where did you come from? he asks with curiosity.

Kate heads off to the cheese room, observing the goings on across the dam as she walks. Her lawyer warned her in August that they had exhausted all legal avenues, so she'd known this would begin sooner rather than later. Yet she cannot accept that one day she will be looking out of her front door at the construction and implementation of a golfing estate.

Loss, she grieves. Loss and damage. Damage and impotence. The invincibility of money. If I had more cash than they do, I could find a way to stop them.

The cheese room door is wide open! Kate quickens her pace. Gert, she suspects. Or perhaps it was her father, starting to wander into places he is not meant to go. But Elihle knows to keep the door closed, she worries, hurrying up the steps. Fortunately the dogs haven't got in, nor the chickens. Thirty kilos of cheese could have been ruined with feathers and dirt, slobber and droppings.

Kate smiles at the thought. Now, *that* could be termed 'organic'. A brand new brand of smelly cheese.

Perhaps it was she who was the last out of the room.

The curd has drained and settled into a firm white block at the bottom of the vat. The thermometer sticks out at an angle reminiscent of shipwreck. Twenty-six degrees. Kate tops up the hot water in the cavity wall. Like humans, these organisms can only function at certain temperatures. She tends them, so they can serve her. Mothering her bacteria.

Kate is aware that she could end up like her father.

They say, if you don't use it, you'll lose it, and farming clearly didn't use what Da needed to keep it. She must start doing Sudoku, crosswords. Or Patience.

Shakes her head at the thought. Monumental waste of time.

Music, she deliberates: Maybe turning again to music will help her retain a functional brain.

Schumann, she remembers, was depressed to the point of suicide, so they stuck him in a mental asylum. Mad, mad decision. A mental asylum in those days was guaranteed to make anyone depressed and suicidal. Berlioz had some sort of schizophrenia. Helfgott, too.

Kate can't think of any musician who had dementia.

Perhaps variety can also keep the connections going. Keep changing your thoughts and attitudes, laying down new neural pathways, leaving the tracks open and unclogged. Avoid chewing on the same old mouldy bone. The brain like a mangy cartoon dog burying an old thought bone, then unearthing and gnawing on it, then burying it again, endlessly insomniac.

She takes the long knife and sinks it into the curd, feeling the almost imperceptible resistance, then the give, until the tip hits the metal base. Efficiently, she starts to section the block into large rectangles.

All at once, she finds herself down on her haunches, holding fast to the side of the tank, the world blurring, nausea pressing into her belly. She feels it in her marrow: They have made the first incision. The surgeons have begun to unpick the seam that tethers her grandchildren to each other. Patiently and painstakingly, over many hours, they will try to undo the terrible error; they will attempt to finish what nature left undone.

There might not be sufficient fabric for two cloths, enough to cover the hurt cut brain, the exposed nerves.

Perhaps this is some grand experiment. A paramedic once told Kate that his lecturer advised their class to do CPR on people who were already dead. He said you can never get enough practice at resuscitation.

Pull yourself together, she commands. Pull yourself up. Stand, and finish dividing the sections. Insert your hand into the clefts, separating the blocks of curd still further. Then slip in the flat of your hand, turn them over one by one so as to extract the last exudate of whey from under the curd's own weight.

Turn your mind over to other things.

Through the window, the three quarter moon with

its moth edge has broken loose from the line of gums. The sky is clear. With any luck the light of the moon will not be obscured tonight.

Beyond the trees, she can see a section of the field on the other side of the dam. The man with the tripod is still in view. Kate wants to swim over and point out to him: There are already four golfing estates in the immediate hundred kilometre stretch of coastline. Four! She wants to ask him: How many are enough?

In the Valley Hotel pub one night, Daniel overheard one of the developers explaining that the local hospitality industry needs to offer what Chinese, American and German golf tourists want: one holiday destination with five different golf courses on five consecutive days.

Kate recalls the evening at Sharon's years ago, where the family celebrated Pesach. She sat and listened to the rhythm of the Hebrew tongue, turning the pages of the prayer book backwards, following in English. She liked the symbolism of the salt and the eggs, she liked the opening of the door to let the spirit of Elijah in, but most of all she loved the traditional song about having enough.

The Jewish prayer celebrated an end to slavery and

expressed gratitude for having sufficient. She joined in the singing: I have food on my plate, it is enough; I have a roof over my head, it is enough; I have clothes on my body, it is enough.

Through the window, the branches are swaying vigorously, despite there being only a slight breeze. Vervet monkeys, scavenging a living in this hominid-dominated landscape.

The clock on the wall shows nine fifty-six. Seven fifty-six there. Kate levers the last of the blocks out, turns it over. Fits it back in between the others. Wash your hands, Kate. She'll be waiting outside the closed theatre doors. Go and phone her now. Do the next right thing.

Down the steps and back along the path. Kate stops. Turns to check: Yes, the cheese room door is closed. She turns again towards the house.

Those that God has joined, let no man put asunder.

Her mind, playing its dirty tricks.

Perhaps there is an old man with a long white beard sitting on a cloud in the sky folding a large piece of paper, then cutting a figure out with scissors, and unfolding it to reveal a string of people joined at the hands and feet, as she used to do as a child. The heads, however, are always separate.

Divorce has its place, also neurosurgery.

Kate and Leonard didn't get married in church; they did it the modern way in the registry office. So full of hope and love and good intentions, like all young newlyweds. Years later, after she stood in court and explained to the judge that their marriage had failed, Leonard phoned her. When I married you, he said, it was for life. His voice had lost its accusatory quality; instead, Kate could hear the shock of the misunderstood child. Kate was also still reeling. She, too, had married for life. Only what they each had understood by marriage and love was different. That's all that happened. That's all.

And now – her thoughts continue, running their way away with her – although they are legally split, sundered, divorced, rifted, bereft, they still have a child. Jess is the bridge that connects them. If it were not for their daughter, she would never see Leonard again. The two of them are forever linked through the inevitable dramas and crises and celebrations of Jess's life, whenever parents are of necessity intimately involved: her birthdays, her own wedding – should she ever have one – the grandchildren, illness and injury.

What a beautiful and terrible thing our daughter embodies, Kate realises, the creative evidence of their love, the tether of their hatred. Poor child, it is too much for anyone to bear. She tore apart, because of her parents, but not down the middle. The bulk of her went over to Leonard. I feel sorry for him, she said; taking sides with the weak one.

Kate stands behind the shed, trying to control her tears. I cannot phone her if I am no good to her.

Jess accuses her mother of not understanding her. But I can't, Kate rails, if you hide yourself from me. You won't even tell me who the father is, she broods, who he is, poor bugger. Was he really so bad, Jess, the one whose seed you accepted?

Her daughter does not trust her. She saw this one morning in Jess's kitchenette, the babies on their backs on the floor chewing rusks. The look in Jess's eyes when she asked her to leave almost killed Kate.

My child, she appeals, centre of my life, we were connected when you were small; we were reflected in each other's eyes. You were both outside of and inside me, simultaneously.

Kate recalls standing through the hot night at the open window, holding her baby daughter upright and asleep against her chest so that the pain in her ear would subside. Holding, rocking, feeding, cleaning – those things that interrupted her life, that supplanted her life, that were her whole life. Jess knows this, now that she has children – practical tending as evidence of love. Kate wonders what her mother went through with her, whether it is the same for all women: a slow acceptance of the decelerated days of wiping snot and living with screaming, with seat-belted journeys, stuck in traffic, nowhere else to go. All gone, all that living and loving and work. All that hard, hard work. Now the empty space, the heart breaking.

I could not love my mother, Kate acknowledges. Jessica can't love me. Betrayal, handed down through the ages.

When they are small, they break your arms; when they are grown, they break your heart. Kate's mum, whispering poison into her daughter's ear. That saying stood in place of her mother trying to understand her, shielded by the great wall of her idioms.

She pulls the screeching screen door open. The surfaces in the kitchen are covered with doughy rounds, their domes sliced lightly twice in parallel lines, ready for the oven. Nine for the guests for lunch, and the rest for the freezer. Nosisi is sprinkling coarse salt and the green twigs of rosemary over them like a blessing.

Kate wants to lie down on her bed, give up for a while. Block her ears against the plaintive sound of engorged goats. She's so tired of being strong and capable, exhausted by this interminable round, coming back every day to the same toothbrush, the same goat.

Perhaps I have cancer, she consoles herself. Now she has imagined such a thing, it will not happen. Only things she hasn't thought of will occur. That is why life is so shocking.

The piano. The telephone. Both silent, waiting.

A piano is pointless without a pianist.

A surgeon is obsolete without a patient.

A mother is redundant without a child.

Somewhere to place your hands.

Already today there has been bleeding, precious life blood lost out of the tiny bodies of her grandsons. Please, she implores, may the surgeons operate with the sensitivity and nuance of great musicians. Or of priests ministering to the temple of the body. Or with the desire of a mother to exorcise her child's pain.

May they understand that what they do is not merely a brilliant technical exercise.

Leonard has informed her that the vasculature of the twin's brains is intertwined. She is inordinately annoyed by this. He knows nothing about biology. He is a language man. It drives her crazy – it's Kate that Jessica should be talking to, she's the one with the MSc.

She fills the glass water bottles and stashes them in the fridge so that they will be cold by lunchtime. Frequently she has to tell guests that she doesn't serve bottled water. Is your water safe to drink? they'll ask, especially the tourists. Yes, she wants to tell them. Fresh rain water off the roof, seasoned with bird droppings, then stored in water tanks and pressure-fed into the taps. We're off the grid here, doing things the old way, no chlorine, no single-use plastic. Just pure adulterated rain water, swimming with the germs you need to be healthy.

A shout outside; Da, yelling: Mary! Mary, you bitch!

It knifes Kate to hear her father speak like that. He never called Mum names when she was alive. Perhaps that's what he really thought of her, the inhibitions of a restrained man dissolving along with his neural tissue. It could just be one of his random word connections misfiring.

Through the French doors and across the lawn, Kate sees the strange duo come into view – Da striding, with Elihle trying to persuade a hat onto the old man's head, as Kate has instructed he should do. Da's bald scalp is a dermatologist's diagnostic delight.

With a flick of annoyance and without halting his pace, Da knocks the hat off. The skin of his crown shines between the patches and knobs of sun damage; his wild eyes are fixed on some inner scenario no one else can fathom.

Elihle gathers up the hat and they pass from view. Sweet young man, I cannot do without him, Kate worries. Perhaps I should adopt him, and leave him the farm in my will.

Kate is left staring at the dam and field beyond, framed by the French doors. The tripod men are no longer around.

She must phone the travel agent. Even Sharon says Jess can't possibly mean it. My daughter is testing me, that's all. I'll go and be on my best behaviour, I'll be gracious to all those women who have taken my place. I will compliment all the surrogate mothers and thank them for taking such good care of my daughter. I will sit with Jess beside her injured children's hospital beds and tell her about the time I sat beside hers. I'll remind her that she chose life, and how grateful I am for that. I will win her back.

The phone rings. It's Sharon. So? Have you heard?

It's too soon. Have you seen what's happened to the exchange rate?

Get that exband of yours to shell out.

I know he'll be there too. With his latest handbag, no doubt.

*Hand*bag! Oh god, Kate! Who is she?

I don't know, nor care.

Of course you do. Tell him not to bring –

He won't listen to me.

Tell Jess to tell him.

She's not going to take my side.

Maybe this isn't about you.

What –?

Maybe Jess is on drugs.

Sharon, you've got drugs on your mind.

I've been going to these meetings, and it's possible, you know. Maybe that was Jess's problem all along.

A clutch of fear in Kate's centre.

I would never admit this –

What?

I checked her room when she was out. I thought maybe the twins were born that way because of, you know, chemicals. I found nothing. No strange packets of powder, no pipes or needles or pills.

That's something.

Look, Sharon, I am in the middle of Cheddaring. Have to go. I'll phone you later, okay?

Okay, Doll. I'm thinking of you all.

It's just past ten.

All is not well.

Springertjie, Kate remembers, is not well.

Going through to the office, she opens a desk drawer and selects a pre-filled syringe, thinking: We are all doing battle with beasts, the inner minotaur and outer bacteria. For this infected teat she has antibiotics, but for the fear that has clamped her by the throat she has no antidote.

Kate has made it this far without antidepressants.

Back along the path: like a parting in green hair, the brown skull of the earth showing through. Like the initial skin incision.

She stops and pulls her jeans down. Crouches,

marking this territory with her urine, her own personal stink. Pity that the Tripods can't smell her little girl wee sprinkled all over her land on the other side of the dam. She brushes herself off with a clutch of grass. Zips up her jeans.

On the phone the other night, Kate's younger sister Pippa reminded her of the mantra she used when her first boyfriend was diagnosed with leukaemia. Tim will be healed, and all will be well. Tim will be healed and all will be well. Tim will be healed and all will be well. Repeated words moving through her like a caress, like a thread threading them through, a lifeline to hold onto in the midst of the helpless sea of fear. And after the treatment, he was well for a while. As though it was the words that had power. As though thoughts and prayer could perform invisible surgery. Kate could not credit that Pippa, with her messed-up life, had a hotline to the numinous.

The couple had a fall out and she broke up with him. A year later, Tim had a relapse and died. Pippa still believes it was her fault.

Kate has tried to find a mantra – a repetitive phrase, a roll of words to bandage up the things in her life that require healing. But she doesn't believe in words.

The surgeons have cut through skin and skull, and are taking up fine instruments to apply to her grandsons' brains.

Humans have agreed to broach, then to breach, the taboo of cutting open another person's living body, both the carver and the carved consenting to participate voluntarily in an act of violence. The knife sliding through skin, violating the integrity of the body. Hurting another with the goal of healing. Permitting a wounding in the hope that the original wound might thereby be cured.

Please god, goddess, she asks, whoever you are, whatever there is: Help us. We are all in terrible need.

There, she has said it.

The goats hear Kate coming and congregate at the gate. She is their goddess, the one who distributes pellets for the belly and scratches for the head. Because of her they live; if she decides, they die. Their yellow eyes protrude from either side of their angular heads; they stare at her with their dark slit pupils as she unties the wire that holds the gate and lets herself in. They press around her, hopeful for morsels. But she is in a hurry, always hurrying through the garden of her life.

Springertjie avoids her, keeping to the edge of the

enclosure as though she knows what's coming. Kate lunges, catches her by a horn and pulls the she-goat towards her. Gert is correct – the end of one teat is red and swollen. Kate swings a leg over the goat's back and clamps her between her knees. Slipping the cover off the needle, she plunges the tip into her buttock muscle. The fluid slides in. A miracle. The she-goat will be better in two days' time, and back to the milking shed within ten. Kate rubs Springertjie's pelt over the puncture, then releases her; she springs about, trying to shake off the ordeal.

You are one lucky goat, Kate tells her. Bacteria killed many great poets and musicians in their prime, robbing the world of their genius – Hopkins, Keats, Chopin, Schubert. But you, you my little goat, have been saved.

There are repeated bouts of hammering from the hok. Kate is pleased to see that Gert is fixing the wooden steps at last.

Will you turn the cheese rounds in the cellar, Gert? She hates asking him anything. He hates her asking, and acquires an aggrieved air. Kate wants to remind him that everyone can do with a bit of reminding. Their little dance.

Ten thirty-three, back to the cheese room. The pyramid cheeses are solidifying nicely. Kate washes and disinfects her hands, and turns the blocks in the vat one by one. The run-off of whey has slowed to a trickle. She picks out a crumb of milk and places it on her tongue. The curd tastes of absolutely nothing now, but with salting and the slow passage of time, it will change from a tasteless rubbery paste into a delicious gastronomic delicacy.

So, patience, Kate, she reminds herself. Take the long view. All things change with the passage of time. Jess will eventually come back to you.

Oh Jess! she weeps, watching a tear splash into the vat; salt from her own grief providing a seasoning for the cheese. She loves and misses that little girl. But the child has gone, gone, and an adult daughter is what she has, or has to grapple with – a woman with her back to her mother.

Her belly announces itself: She has to shit. Back to the house, wading through the day, then to the guest toilet so she doesn't have to look at the damp in the en-suite bathroom.

She remembers Gert as a young man chasing an escaped goat across their neighbour's land and the beating he gave the animal when he caught her. He didn't have proper fencing then, and goats are as crafty as Houdini. Those days, he lived on the other side of the dam with his family in one of the labourers' cottages, which Kate hears Leisure Consortium has started renovating into an ethnically up-market sales office. Gert had started keeping a few goats, in the face of Da's ridicule, but Da did agree to help fence them in under threat from Wilhelm's father next door. During her school holidays, Kate would visit Gert to help with the milking, also to beg for a sliver of his soft white cheese with a satin covering of fungus which he would hold out to her on the edge of his knife.

Missie Kate, he would pronounce, as though he was a priest delivering the sacrament, You are tasting a piece of heaven.

So different from shop-bought cheeses. Chalk and cheese, Kate smiles. Haha!

This man, who only achieved a standard five, humbled her when she took over the farm, proving that her expensive university education was deficient in knowledge – an MSc in microbiology pitted against folk wisdom concerning cultures and curd, time and temperature. Jy kannie dit forseer nie, he would tell his employer, as she tried to manipulate the brew with imported moulds and bacteria. Die kaas weet wat moet gebeur. Moenie fiddle nie, laat los!

When she took his advice, the cheese went on to win prizes, first at local cheese shows and then at an international competition for cheese made from raw milk in Lyon, France.

Kate is only too aware that she has resources of land and transport and a driving licence and bank loans and marketing skills and communication systems and contacts, but she could not have achieved her success without Gert, despite all her training.

She stands and flushes, and watches the turd swill and disappear. At least here, unlike in the city, this water and excrement goes back into the soil via a septic tank with the help of micro-organisms. This thought consoles her.

She is in need of consolation.

Kate washes her hands again, then goes through to the kitchen for a quick cuppa. Nosisi is out in the garden cutting small posies for the tables. Sprigs of lavender and rosemary to enchant the anticipatory olfactory nerve.

An empty bottle of dishwashing liquid is left

standing on the table, Nosisi's reminder for the shopping list. Kate makes a mental note and deposits the plastic bottle into the bin. Closes the lid. Out of sight, out of mind. Rubbish out in the road is more honest, she believes, a reminder that there are consequences to the way we live.

Our grandchildren will regard the commonplace practices of our time with disbelief, she thinks, as we have done regarding our predecessors. Slavery was once an unquestioned part of the economy.

You're raving. Jessica's annoyed voice, come to chide her mother. Stop raving.

But these thoughts obsess me, retorts Kate. Damage to the mother. The earth and all her living things.

The kettle has boiled. She hopes that coffee, with its toasted bean fragrance, will help her out of the gloom.

Nosisi comes in, clutching fragrant bunches of green and purple. Kate asks something that has been playing on her mind: Sisi, has Elihle been to initiation yet?

She shakes her head. That boy must go soon, she emphasises. He is old, almost nineteen. He was busy with his parents, and now –

She leaves the gap for Kate to think about, while

she fills small bottles with water for the table posies: Elihle is too busy caring for Da to undertake his cultural duty.

And there is the money, Nosisi continues, sighing. He has no family to help him.

Nosisi is telling Kate it is her fault that Elihle has not yet become a man. I could help him with money, she reflects, or a sacrificial goat, but what would I do if he took the required time off? Even I cannot take a few weeks off. The old ways do not fit the modern timetable.

Priority: She must get back to the cheese room. She drinks down the last of the coffee and deposits the mug in the sink on her way out.

The harem of hens scatter in their jerky flustered, exclaiming way as she steps out of the door. The rooster draws himself up to full height and releases a volley of crows, his whole body involved in generating the loud, strained sounds, his fleshy comb jigging on his crown. Then he leaps upon a hen's back, and presses her forcefully to the ground for extra territorial effect, scraping a few of her dorsal feathers out with his spur. When he is done, he struts off, and the hen resumes her pecking.

Life without frontal lobes, reflects Kate. The evolution of the prefrontal cortex in human beings was supposed to provide executive functions – planning, restraint and good judgement. Yet this development does not seem to have decreased abuse.

It is something one has to practice, perhaps, the insertion of choice between impulse and action, or between imposition and yielding. The realisation that abuse of self, others, animals or the earth can be shifted towards a different ending.

In the postgrad research lab, the baby mice were sexed soon after birth and the males put to death. The lab manager explained that male mice were too aggressive to be used in experiments. Only female mice were docile and compliant enough to allow themselves to be cooped up, bored, pricked, shocked, have tubes stuck into various orifices, and have the top of their heads sliced off so that electrodes could be inserted into their brains. The few females that displayed any sign of distress or desire to escape were labelled difficult. Kate requested a transfer to the *E.coli* lab.

Kate herself has been called 'difficult'. She regards it as a compliment.

Ten fifty-six. Squirt of alcohol, a wash of the hands, and she begins to turn the blocks of curd again.

There's that old feeling from her childhood, like a beggar out in the cold looking through the window at a lit family scene. That time Beth became ill and was kept at home on the farm while Kate was sent back to boarding school, despite her own aching and protesting tummy. Lying in her bed in the long, cold dormitory rows at night, she wept to think of her sister at home in front of the fire, swaddled in love, warmed by their parents' devoted gaze. Kate hoped Beth would die so that Da and Mum might turn and notice her. After a term, Beth got better, and without any warning, a new baby arrived. Her parents' attention swivelled off Beth, right over Kate's head, all the way round onto the cute new Pippa.

Leonard and his latest girlfriend will apply the poultice of their caring attention onto Jessica and her predicament. The two of them will move in and take up the parental space. Kate will be left cold-shouldered.

Give me another chance, she appeals to her child. I want to put things right. There were many moments when mothering overwhelmed her. The endlessly repeating tasks of nappies and bottles, of uniforms and lunch boxes, of bath and meal times, of the questioning, demanding child. Living life in service of the child, while her own self was neglected. Grateful for the electronic babysitter – the mesmerising television screen sopping up Jessica's scattered focus for long enough for Kate to reassemble herself, and read, or sit in the luxury of quiet immobility and her own unencumbered thought. Pushing her child away – go and play – or trying to keep her quiet with books or blocks or a walk to the park, because Daddy was preparing a lecture or writing his next novel.

Writing! While her sheet music turned yellow in the drawer: notes lying still and silent on the page while fish moths busied themselves, eating études, editing Mozart.

Or she was alone at home with Jess while Leonard was out doing a reading, or a creative writing workshop – settings for seducing women. Abandoned to her insecurity, incapacity and fear, and her haphazard attempts at mothering, out of that pathetic place of waiting for her husband to come home.

Now there is no philandering husband to accuse, and still she is full of error.

Jess is a surprisingly able mother. Kate watched how her daughter got down to the level of the twins, getting around their disability by playing and crawling with them on the carpet, and lying next to them on the bed, singing them rhymes and playing with their fingers and toes. Teasing them with peek-a-boo. Cuddling them as best she could. Kissing them from one mouth to the other like a windscreen wiper, slowly, then quicker, making funny sounds as she did so, to shrieks of their merriment. Only once during the two weeks Kate was visiting did she see her daughter snap at them, jigging their cot to the chorus of their wails when Storm would not sleep and kept waking Sky.

One morning, when there was a gap in the rain, Kate took the twins out in the pram under the sulky English firmament. While walking along the Thames, a homely middle-aged woman slowed down to lean into the pram, her face full of delighted anticipation. Kate stiffened as she watched the woman's expression change to one of shock. Confronted by the woman's horrified face, Sky's eyes widened and filled, and he began to wail, then Storm started to scream and kick. The woman flashed a tense smile. Lovely weather we're having, she offered, pretending she hadn't noticed, and hurried on.

Kate turned the large and awkward pram around and headed back to the flat, pushing her cartload of deformed grandchildren in front of her, wanting to get away from the ignorant public as fast as she could. The babies were winding themselves up into a frenzy, twisting around in the pram, trying to escape the harness that held them, their clenched fists waving, their red faces crumpled and sweating. If they were normal, if there was only one of them crying, she would know what to do. She would pick the child up, and comfort him, as she had done with Jess. She would distract him by holding him close and pointing out the flowers bursting with indigo, and the butterflies floating on the breeze like fragments of light silk cloth.

Jess, who was supposed to be taking a nap, heard them coming a block away. She came through the lobby and out into the street. What happened? she accused her mother. They have never cried like this before!

Back in the flat, she got the twins out of the pram, into her bedroom and onto her bed. While Kate was putting the kettle on, she heard the door close. The babies were calming down as their mother sang to them, crooned and called them by their pet names, Ky-ky, and Big Boy.

Kate stood in the horrid melamine open-plan kitchen amongst pegged washing, unwashed bowls and scattered toys, her heart hammering against her chest. For the first time in ten years she felt like having a cigarette. She marched to Jess's bedroom door and flung it open. Do you want some tea? she asked.

Her daughter, sitting on the bed, bent over her half-whimpering, half-gurgling sons, glared up at her: Just give me a moment, won't you?

Kate turns the last of the blocks and leans her outstretched arms on the edge of the vat, bowing her head. She is strapped to this story, and must endure it.

A phone is ringing in the house, then it stops. Nosisi calls in her urgent, full voice. Kate runs from the room, remembers to look back midstride and shoves the cheese room door closed.

The grass has dried in the sunshine, and the ridges of mud in the driveway are firming up.

Who is it? she calls as she enters the house.

Nosisi is taking a handful of cutlery to the tables on the stoep. Pippa, she says. You must phone at twelve, she is working.

Pippa claims telepathy, yet needs to use a landline.

When her younger sister was seven, she set out to find the end of the rainbow. After dusk, Farmer Jan found her lost and crying, and brought her home. That didn't stop her believing in illusions.

Kate takes a large bowl out to the veggie patch to harvest salad leaves from the garden, the sweet, peppery and tangy mixtures of rocket, mustard and butter lettuce. She pinches them off and tosses them into the bowl. Nine guests for lunch today: three tourists from France staying at the Lodge down the road; and Oom Fanie from over the berg, come to show off the local haute cuisine to his city relatives. Organic goat's milk cheese and salad, and home-baked bread. People travel far for what Kate offers.

There is an abundance of growth in the salad garden

after the rains. Satisfaction sprouts in Kate as she bends and picks. The young green leaves of spinach squeak in her hands.

Pippa calls herself a healer, trained by a guru in India. The family thought she was a masseuse until their godmother Margaret went to see her. She phoned Kate, shocked by what she described as pornographic posters adorning Pippa's walls. Kate left work early and drove across town to her sister's home.

A brass plaque was screwed onto the wall beside the front door: Pippa Newman, Tantric Massage Practitioner. Kate has an MSc in genetics and microbiology and had worked for years to help infertile couples in a top in-vitro fertilisation lab, but she had never had a brass plaque.

She pointed a finger and pressed the bell. The door opened to a cloud of incense and Indian music and a couple of escaping cats. There stood, not Pippa, but a good-looking young man in a long white caftan, with eyeliner on the edges of his eyelids. He put his hands together and performed a little bow.

That was Jerome, the man who later stole Pippa's CD collection of Indian raga music and ran off with her boyfriend. Before these calamities, Pippa had introduced him as her spiritual pupil, sent by her Indian guru to do part of his apprenticeship with her.

I am so pleased you've come! said Pippa. So you can understand what I do. People are so misinformed.

Margaret's complaint of pornography referred to the stylised posters of oriental men and women in various sexually gymnastic positions on the walls of Pippa's consulting room. Above a shrine hung a drawn image, intricately decorated, of a huge erect phallus on the verge of penetrating a florid and descending yoni, folding open like a large bud. The room was soft with exotic furnishings, lit candles and a double bed spread with white sheets.

On a wooden box next to the door was a notice: 'Your donation, please. According to your income. For reference: A doctor's consultation is currently R250 for fifteen minutes.'

The truth broke through Kate's carefully constructed notions of how the world works. The little girl who used to climb onto her lap, mesmerised, for yet another telling of *The Little Mermaid*, sat straight-backed, adorned and spangled, and told Kate proudly that she was a member of the International Society of Tantric Sex and Massage Practitioners.

The ubiquitous problem of snails. Kate plucks one off the lettuce leaf as it rapidly disappears into its rasping maw, feeling the resistant suck of its foot as the creature tries to hold fast to its food and life, then shrinks quickly back into its shell, its second survival strategy. She recalls her distaste in first year zoology, pinning out the loop of a snail's digestive tract onto the dissection board. She's read that a hatred of snails is a hatred of women, a disgust of those sensitive and delicate mucoid folds.

She cannot think of that now, for her lettuce is disappearing fast.

Pippa explained that becoming initiated into the mysteries of sacred sexuality was not only about sex. Male and female energies are very different, she said. Some clients who come for healing want a man to work with and some a woman.

Jerome and I protect each other, she said. There are some weird people out there, you know, she warned, her eyes widening.

Oh, Pippa, despairs Kate, always attracted to lost creatures, mad about men and cats, rescuing them, taking them home, crying over them.

Once they had started getting involved with boys,

Kate and her friends would return to boarding school and ask each other: How far did you go? Did you kiss? *Tongue* kiss? Did he touch your boobs? Or (giggle) *down there*? Have you touched his? Did you actually *see* it? Much falling about. Did you go *all the way*?

Most of this had been only talk – girls wanting and fearing the controversial status that an active sex life conferred.

Kate was not able to bring herself to ask Pippa how far, and with which part of her anatomy, does she go in her sessions, hoping that only her sister's hands were involved.

Kate is embarrassed to admit that she did notice Jerome's hands, she could not help it, pressed as they were like an ongoing prayer in front of his chest. His fingers were long and sensitive like a musician's. She was suffused by a vigorous and alarming desire for those hands to lay themselves upon her, wakening the act of carefully, wildly, taking a man into her centre. An astonishing act of trust and hope and relief. And of exquisite, unimaginable pleasure.

If you do not have it, there is nothing you can do about it, she mourns. There are substitutes like the terrible purple dildo Sharon gave her for her birthday.

It sounded like a vacuum cleaner when it was switched on. Some things you cannot buy, she knows, like a respectful and present and playful lover who values you, one who wants the best for you, and will give and take in equal measure. Who wants to work things out in bed and out of it. Who is able to stand up and stand down. Who is interested not only in the momentary act but the continuum of making love, making a life of depth where love grows slowly like the maturing of curd, from the innocence and ignorance of milk into something satiating, solid, sturdy. A nourishment to share.

Da, from the direction of the shed, calling – Mary! Mary! – imprisoned by the chain of synapses firing in the same sequence day after day.

The snails are also in the mustard lettuce. Gert has not put down sufficient tobacco dust to deter them. He does not see the point of eating leaves. Kate feels for the hard fruit of a carapace concealed beneath the light green foliage, and wonders whether she should add garlic snails to the menu.

When Jessica was small, she decided that God

was like a snail. What do you call it? she asked. Hermaphrodite, my darling. God, to her beautiful child's beautiful mind, was both. Now she believes what has been written down by men in a book.

The snails feel like berries between her fingertips, their sheathed bodies rolling into her cupped palm as she plucks them, then drops them to the ground and crushes them beneath her gumboot. Every time the shell cracks open like a soft nut, she imagines the broken edge slicing into fragile tissues, and there is a recoil in her chest akin to a small grief or horror. As she grinds her heel down, she sees the intricate respiratory, circulatory and digestive tracts mushing together into a terrible paste. All that hard-earned body gone to waste.

She is moved to address them: Dear snails, let me apologise. We are all just trying to survive. And I suffer from an overdeveloped sense of sympathy, a sentimentality of the heart in constant opposition to the brutality of the head.

What God has joined, let no man put asunder.

The refrain of her fettered brain has again come to mock her. In her second year, she was stunned by the beauty of the stained histology slide, all the connections of nerves and tendons, ligaments and sheaths. Kate knows she is guilty, that her path is littered with corpses. She has destroyed many things that she never could have made. This farming life has entailed cutting a swathe of death.

She wants absolution, not only for murdering snails.

Eleven twenty-seven. They are two-and-a-half hours into the operation.

Leonard will use this event as material for his next book, taking notes, jotting things down. It's how Kate found out that he was cheating on her. The way he wrote about sex in *The Fairest Way*, she knew he hadn't made it up. In the novel, a woman named Melody would tongue stories of anonymous and group sex into the protagonist's orgasmic ear while they rocked in first this position, then that.

When Kate confronted him, he accused her of reading things into the text and being envious of his writing life. She believed him for a while, flagellating herself for being jealous of his women friends, of his writing success. Until she discovered that there was a real Melody, and went round to her house one night and found Leonard's combi in her driveway. Kate kept ringing the doorbell until Melody answered. When she tried to close the door, saying Leonard wasn't there, Kate pushed past her and found him in her bed.

There are techniques in life that are underutilised, Kate notes. The reality check for example.

She nips off a few buds from the tomato bushes to encourage the best crop and goes over to the weir at the stream to rinse the greens. A frog plops into the water, then floats spread-limbed and unmoving as death, trying to deceive her eye. Don't be alarmed, she reassures her. Although the French are my guests today, I will refrain from serving your legs.

Poor Melody. A year later she arrived at Kate's front door with flowers nestling in an exquisite vase. I'm sorry, she wept, and described how Leonard had cheated on her in turn.

If you wait on the bridge long enough, the bodies of your enemies come floating by. A favourite piece of old Chinese wisdom that Leonard used to quote when they first met. Melody was one of several corpses that had drifted past under Kate's bemused eye, all incumbents who thought they were the special one, the one Leonard would change for, the one he would never cheat on. They had all come past on the river of their own tears.

Kate knew from the beginning that Leonard had cheated on his girlfriends, yet she'd believed he would change. He had hoped Kate would alter her attitude to accommodate threesomes. Neither of them had. Neither wanted to lay down new neural tissue in the direction of the other's need.

She shakes the droplets from the leaves, noting that water was valuable when humans walked to the river to fetch and carry it home. Every drop was precious. Now, taps leak. We throw good water down the drain. We waste it by weeping over reality.

One foot in front of the other. Eleven forty-three. Just over an hour to go before the guests arrive, but Kate must first finish with the cheese.

The kitchen is sated with the smell of home-baked bread and the sensory intrusion of the daily radio soap that Nosisi listens to – a love story spiced with envy and betrayal which ends at twelve, blurring into news headlines.

Nosisi is saying something in isiXhosa to Elihle through the window. Kate catches the word for 'today' and the word for 'finished'. These intimate black strangers who live inside white lives.

It's twelve, Nosisi points out.

Kate nods. By not phoning Pippa, she is still punishing her sister for suggesting that Kate's marital problems were rooted in her base chakra. Besides, she dislikes phoning. Those years locked away in boarding school, when the pay phone the only way to escape the school property during term time, the occasional forced conversation with her parents, always pointless and depressing.

There are enough tomatoes in the bowl on the counter – the bowl she bought at Sharon's Raku exhibition. Put the leaves in the lettuce spinner, which was a gift from her mother when she moved out of this home, never imagining she would return. Plates from her childhood with the repeating pattern. The oak dresser with ceramic handles, a remnant of her time with Leonard. Kate's world is filled with fragments of her past, dragged together and stacked around her like a rampart.

Arrange the leaves on the plates and fetch cheeses from the fridge. Lean on the knife with both hands, slice the truckle of Cheddar into aesthetic wedges and place them on the leaves, together with halves of Provolone and scoops of soft goat's milk cheese, the effect completed by the pyramid cheeses, cherry tomatoes and home-made fig preserve, and garlic- and chilli-impregnated olives. Abundant luxury. Verdant earth. A serving of manna, nourishment for the whole being, fallen from the heaven of Kate's hands.

No time now to cut the marinated pears for the dessert. Kate asks Nosisi to do this, then heads back to the cheese room. The clouds have dispersed; no sign of the predicted scattered showers. The dam water ripples, cool and inviting. But the deep also contains this morning's dream image of a drowning girl.

Luzoko is the one who cannot swim, despite Kate's encouragement and offers to teach him. Like his mother, he is afraid of deep water. Yet he is not afraid of an unsterile knife applied to his most sensitive skin with no anaesthetic. The bandage, Nosisi told her, is made of mielie leaves tied in place with a leather thong to stem the blood and approximate the edges of the cut. Sounds like a painful option that would chafe and increase the chances of infection. Those who wield the knife have suffered themselves. Sink or swim, that is the maxim. Those who survive the ordeal probably apply the knife with zeal.

It occurs to her that these boys bleed from their cut genitals as girls do when they pass into adulthood.

Dear Luzoko, happiest when dancing a soccer ball between his feet. Only recently, he was showing Elihle tricks with his fancy footwork until Brutus sank his teeth into the plastic. Today, he is sitting somewhere in the bush, waiting through pain to be accepted as a man.

The sun sears the back of her neck. She promises herself a swim once the guests have gone, but perhaps the dream was a warning: a post-prandial cramp, a quick submersion. Death flooding in, displacing life.

She wonders whether nocturnal chemical events can prophesy and prognosticate. Kate was sitting at Mary's bedside when she stopped breathing just before three o'clock. When she phoned Pippa with the news, her baby sister told her she'd woken at four minutes past three, having dreamt that their mother had come round to say goodbye before catching a train to Siberia.

Back in the cheese room, Kate stacks the blocks of curd into a double layer as she turns them to increase the pressure and extract the whey.

At least Mum and Da were spared the details of Pippa's life, Mum retreating into death and Da into dementia. Kate doesn't know whether her sister is fucked in the head or a post-modern saint – the New Agers annexing the massage parlour as a spiritual path. A logical extension of incorporating the stripper's pole routine into the gym workout of the modern housewife.

Pippa insists that sex and sexuality have been so brutalised and commodified that humans have lost connection with its sacred essence. All she is offering is a path towards sexual healing beyond the ravages of shame. She explained patiently to Kate that we were all hurt sexually and many of us sexualised our hurts.

The dogs start up, barking as they rush down the drive. Above their din there is the rattle of Daniel's bakkie, arriving to fetch the whey. This is not a good moment. Annoyed, Kate watches him draw up. He pushes his large frame out of the cab, holding something in his fist. He often brings Kate offerings from his garden. Today, he presents a bunch of radishes, freshly pulled from the ground, small amounts of earth still adhering to the fine roots. She accepts them, ashamed, grateful that someone in this remote part of the world thinks of her amidst the round of life. He adores her, which assigns her to a slightly unstable platform that could tip at any moment. There is plenty about her that is not adorable, she knows.

An overweight, sweaty man, anxious to please. A man with an ordinary face; not a seducer. Kate wonders whether that is why she has not fallen for him. Perhaps she only falls for damaged men. But then, we are all damaged, Daniel too, she sighs. He displays evidence of his weakness for the world to see, under the taut skin of his torso.

Daniel pulls Kate to him, pressing her body into his belly. It feels as though he has inserted a cushion between them. He looks into her face. Any news? he asks, concerned. He has kind eyes, couched in soft folds. It would be possible, she thinks, to kiss him between the eyes.

No, it's too soon. I have so much to do if I go, it's a bit overwhelming.

Can I do anything, I mean, to help? Sweet Daniel, always offering. He is lonely, living with his pigs. Over Daniel's shoulder, Kate sees Da's emaciated form pitching itself towards them from the direction of the dam, Elihle following. Her father should be asleep by now. The guests are about to arrive and she cannot have any further disturbances nor embarrassments.

The two of them appear at Daniel's side. Did you – Kate starts, but Elihle shakes his head with what looks like irritation. The angel is taking strain.

I gave him his tablets. They're not working yet.

Da is a little subdued, but the dose of sedative Dr Harris prescribes to help the situation through lunchtime usually knocks him right out. His brain is no longer able to restrain him, so Kate has to when necessary, with the aid of medication.

Morning, Mr Newman, Daniel says, offering his hand. They have been neighbours for at least ten years, yet Da looks at Daniel's hand, puzzled. Either he has forgotten who Daniel is, or he has lost the ritual of social convention.

Aren't you tired, Da? Kate's anxiety is climbing. Da lost it badly a year ago when he ordered lunch guests out of the house, roaring and overturning a laden table, not unlike Jesus evicting the money changers from the temple.

Mary left it in America, Da reports from the strange planet of his mind. In the green cupboard.

He begins to cry. This from a man whose wife said

that he never cried, not even when his mother was murdered on an ordinary morning walk along the cliffs near her home on the coast, a few years before Kate was born. Now he cries often, the dam of his feelings breached.

I'll take him, Daniel offers. He has stepped in once before, removing Da from the house before lunch when Kate's father flushed his tablets down the toilet one Saturday, and Dr Harris was not contactable.

Relief lifts her. You are the best. Elihle, please help Daniel with the whey, then you can go along too.

Guilt ruffles round in her, so she offers Daniel recompense: Come for supper? she says, and immediately regrets it. She can't be with anyone today.

Daniel nods happily, and she reprimands herself for being churlish.

Great. See you later.

Making supper for a wonderful friend, sharing good food and wine and heartache at the end of a difficult day. These small human acts are important.

I'll bring pudding! he adds.

Pudding is the last thing on her mind, the first on his. She nods, and strides away down the path.

Nosisi is laying tables. Twelve twenty-nine. Kate's

body is tensing with the pressure of time; how to get through the day faster, with a sensation of wading through thigh-deep wet cement. The pressure of her bladder will have to wait. Clear the kitchen table and roll out the cheese cloth, measuring and cutting enough to line the stainless steel truckle mould. Leave Nosisi to clear up. She takes the mould and salt down to the cheese room.

Daniel is driving off with Da and Elihle squashed beside him in the cab, the dogs giving chase. Daniel waves through the window, and she raises her hand in reply, thinking: We are strange creatures, living a handmade life. At least we should give each other a little comfort.

She enters the cheese room and throws a handful and a half of salt into the vat, and starts to break up the blocks of curd, mixing in the salt. Taking the cheese cloth, she lines the truckle mould, then packs the salted curd into it as quickly as possible. Twelve fifty-five. She hopes the guests will be late, but no, there's the sound of a vehicle and the dogs barking again. Through the doorway, she sees Oom Fanie's van coming up the drive. Nosisi will have to welcome them.

Scrape up the last of the curd in her cupped hand,

throw it into the container, then close up the top with cheesecloth and insert the lid. Where the hell is Gert? He could be of more efficient help. The problem of authority.

Gert! Kate calls from the door. There he is, walking over from the shed. He comes up the steps, avoiding his employer's eyes, and helps her move the heavy container onto the press. They position it, then Kate starts rotating the wheel that lowers the sliding lid down onto the cylinder of curd. Whey spouts and trickles out of the pores punctured into the bottom of the container.

Totsiens, Missie Kate. Gert nods, impatient, taking his cap from behind the door. Kate has forgotten: Today is Wednesday, Gert's half-day. This day of all days she needs support. On Wednesdays and Saturdays, she must milk the goats herself in the evening. She casts wildly about in her mind, seeking an excuse or escape. Perhaps she should bribe him with a fistful of notes. But he is already walking away, lighting up. Kate is too proud to call after him, or too tired. She reasons: It's good, I need to keep busy on a day such as this.

One last turn of the wheel, and she is off to see to the

guests. Here comes the other car, the French in a four-by-four, come to conquer Africa. Kate strides forward, aware of looking the part – old jeans, gumboots, T-shirt, with one-time sexy tan blotching into aging, sun-damaged skin at the vee of her shirt.

The skin on her mother's bum, which never once saw the sun, was still as soft as a baby's at seventy-one. Kate marvelled at this while sitting on the edge of her sick bed, rubbing her hip and back. Metastases, those cells whose DNA is as scrambled as Da's brain, had gone amok, eroding her mother's bone and causing her agony. Even morphine was not enough. Kate rubbed and rubbed, trying to erase her mother's suffering. It's like toothache of the hip, she complained.

Good afternoon! Bon après-midi! Kate greets the three men who are getting out of their vehicle. They grip her hand in turn, intoning greetings in their sing-song nasal French. How differently people shake hands, Kate notes. The older one with a manicured grey beard gives her only the tips of his fingers as though she might be offering him something contagious, the middle-aged, balding one hurts her slightly with his enthusiasm, and the young, middle-eastern looking one takes her hand in both of his and brushes his lips against the back of her wrist, perhaps to atone for his companions' insensitivity. So much character concentrated in this single gesture.

She ushers them into the house, glancing briefly at herself in the hall mirror and running fingers through her hair while they exchange a few stock English pleasantries, then takes them through to a table on the stoep that overlooks the dam. The breeze has died completely and the still water replicates the mountains in soft blue hues like a colour-enhanced photograph. 'Idyllic, tranquil', the local restaurant guide describes this vista. Her restaurant has won local awards two years running. The Frenchmen seat themselves and lapse into their native tongue, a language that lends itself to dramatic gesture. Already Kate has a story about these three. The young man's accent is not convincing. She suspects he is an immigrant, fallen in with an older couple. They adore him; he has resurrected their interest in life, in sex. Even in each other. They live together in a large king-size bed in the centre of Paris, the young one in the middle.

From the table on the side stoep, she hears Oom Fanie recounting one of his stories and his guests laughing – female laughter.

Kate offers the wine menu to the oldest-looking of the triumvirate, but the balding one lifts it neatly out of her grasp. She waits for an objection, but the grey beard acquiesces. She has misread the hierarchy.

She explains that she serves only local wines and that they are excellent. The bald one chooses a Sauvignon Blanc. On the way to the fridge, she stops briefly to greet the guests at Oom Fanie's table, where he is sitting with four women and a prepubescent girl of about nine years old. He introduces them, ending with the tiny woman with dyed bright red hair sitting next to him whose knee has been captured by his hand. This, he tells Kate proudly through teeth so perfect they can only be dentures, is his new girlfriend. She looks astonishingly similar to his recently dead wife. The woman grimaces, but Kate understands that this is the way she smiles, an obedient crumpling of the face. The redhead deposits her hand dryly, apologetically, in Kate's for a moment.

Nosisi is placing cheese platters in front of the Frenchmen as she returns with the wine. They have begun an altercation, the grey beard objecting in flurried French to something the young man has said. Kate hopes that the wine will render them mellow rather than increasingly belligerent. One never knows which way it will go with alcohol.

The younger man turns to her. His face has hardened, become more determined. Tell me, he asks, what are these people walking with er, the blanket? And the painted faces?

Nosisi pauses to listen on her way to the kitchen. Kate finishes pouring the wine into his glass, twisting the bottle to prevent drops landing on the cloth, then explains: They are Xhosa boys undergoing traditional initiation. Where did you see them?

Greybeard butts in: On the pass we stopped today. We saw three below the bridge, but when they saw us, they went away, vite, vite. He flicks his hand to indicate their haste.

They object to the photos, the young one insists. They are not animals in a zoo.

But nobody said they are animals! The older man gestures with exasperation. People are taking photos all the time, of anybody and anything!

They aren't allowed contact with other people during initiation, Kate offers as an explanation that might save the lunch. The white clay on their faces is also meant to conceal them from other people's eyes.

They are busy with a sacred thing, yes? insists the young man, appealing to her. It is like barging into a mosque with your camera. He makes soft explosive sounds with his lips: Pah! Pah! Pah! while holding up his hands and flicking his fingers, camera flashlights going off.

Were they all right?

The men swivel round to see who asked. Nosisi says again: Did they look well?

One wagtail sign is not enough to get a mother through a difficult day.

They look like ghosts! Greybeard laughs. Maybe they are already dead.

Nosisi turns back to the kitchen. Kate hesitates, wanting to explain to these foreigners that one of the initiates is Nosisi's son. But the moment has passed and the bald one is lifting his glass of wine, toasting her. Very good wine! Your country, it is full of surprises.

Kate has to agree, then goes after Nosisi, wanting to comfort her. But Nosisi has busied herself with a knife, cutting pieces off the homemade block of butter, transferring them into small stainless steel pots, then levelling the rich yellow substance to a smooth surface.

The batter still needs to be made, so Kate fetches eggs from the basket.

Those Frenchmen, Kate tries, speaking quietly so that her voice does not carry to the stoep. They are ignorant.

Nosisi grunts, keeping her eyes on her task.

They didn't mean it, you know, they weren't trying to be unkind.

Nosisi puts down the knife and glares at her employer. Taking, always taking, she says, drying her hands on a tea towel, and carries the boards with fresh loaves and pots of butter out to the guests. Kate has started beating the batter by the time she returns with the beverage order for Oom Fanie's table. Diet Coke and Fanta. While eating gourmet cheese. Kate shudders, and decides she will no longer stock soda drinks.

Her employee seems to have recovered from the Frenchman's faux pas. Kate wants to remind her that one has to handle all characters when running a restaurant. Can't take anything too personally.

Going back outside, Kate tops up the wine at the French table. The tension has eased. Greybeard asks Kate to take a photo of the three of them, arm in arm, leaning their butts against the balustrade, with the dam and the mountains behind them. The young one is in the middle, with the two older men looking down at him with fond amusement.

Say cheese, Kate suggests, her usual quip when performing this task for happy-snapping trippers, but these three do not appear to have come across the idiom before. She depresses the button and the shot freezes on the camera screen. The three of them will forever look puzzled. Well and good, she thinks. Africa is puzzling. She wants to laugh as she hands the camera back. Saying 'fromage' as the shot is taken wouldn't create the same faked expression of pleasure as the English word achieves. Before she is required to explain her odd command, she returns to the kitchen. Sits to take the weight off her aching feet and back, turns to beating the batter.

Through the side door, just out of sight, Fanie is impressing his guests with stories about the wonderful way the district is being upgraded – wider roads, new sporting facilities, golf courses and hotels. He emphasises how good it is for the local economy.

Fanie's granddaughter interests Kate. She can see her through the door while she prepares the pancakes.

The girl has curly brown hair scraped back and tamed by a blue Alice band, and metal strips that clamp her teeth. She is looking away at the tangle of indigenous bush, sitting on her hands as though to quieten them. But her legs will not be still, they are swinging impatiently on the hinge of her knees.

It occurs to Kate that she would rather be dancing. The girl doesn't care about the painstakingly prepared and beautifully presented food that Nosisi is placing in front of her. She would rather move in a dream across a wide sprung floor, her torso sylph-like, her body anointing the space with breath and grace.

No, it's not that, for now she has pulled a sketchbook from a sling bag hanging from her chair and has placed it on her lap below the table top. Her hand grips a pencil, the pencil tip is arcing across the blank page. The girl's whole body is bent and aligned to this task. Kate sees that another world has shifted her out of this time and place and into its own circumstance. She has heard a call, insistent and clear, that the rest of her family is deaf to. The girl is immersed in recording an image unfolding before her inner eye. She bows her head in reverence, in service to her art.

Kate longs to look over her shoulder, wanting to

follow the quick strokes and long lines that describe an inner life.

The girl is so preoccupied she does not hear the bark assailing her: Oom Fanie is telling her not to be rude. The woman sitting next to her, presumably her mother, snatches the pencil away and scolds the girl for not obeying her grandfather. Her face lifts, shocked out of the dreamy deep, slashed with incomprehension as though injured by this abrupt crash back into the violence of the world; her mouth open, her hand lifting to try to regain the tool that means more to her than food or shelter, for this is her food and shelter: the pencil with which she catches the image, transcribing those things that fascinate and disturb her through lines and shade and light.

Her body follows her hand, rising out of her chair, reaching for the pencil, the lifeline that can help reveal her to herself. The tool she may not have, for her mother and her grandfather have deemed other things more important.

Oom Fanie reiterates: Tanya, hou op. Dis nie tyd vir speletjies nie. Eet jou kos. The woman next to her confiscates the sketchbook as well; impounds it under her chair. It lies on the floor, a mere rectangle.

The child dwindles onto her seat, her eyes slide; she forks listlessly at a wedge of cheese, but Kate is on her feet, wanting to stride onto the stoep and invite the girl to come and sit beside her in the kitchen with her sketchbook and take all the time in the world to follow her impulse into image. Kate wants to observe how this child folds the task about her, how she cloaks herself in the silk of desire.

Kate recognises her; she was like this – once.

I want this for myself, she yearns.

Kate longs to feel the ecstasy of Brahms running through her fingers, swelling the air with exquisite overlays of sound. She has never known such union as those times when she forgot her struggling intention and found herself both lost and found inside the music.

There were certain other occasions: while making love, and when she first held her new-born daughter.

Tanya is eating dutifully, without relish. Order and politeness at table have been restored. There is nothing to be done without making a fuss. Life is like this: We must not make a fuss.

The batter is the right consistency. Get the cream from the fridge.

Nosisi is quieter than usual as she wipes down the kitchen counters. Have you had something to eat? Kate checks, her own stomach complaining.

I ate earlier.

I should have baked you a cake.

You should have. Nosisi's tone is ambiguous.

I'll make you an extra big pancake. You're fifty-three, right? I don't have enough candles. It will have to be pancake flambé, one huge flame for your life, no candles.

Nosisi nods and gathers up the baking trays, taking them through to the scullery for washing.

Jessica once sat at this same kitchen table at about the same age as Tanya, refusing to eat her food. Now her golden daughter has gone, forsaken her.

No, Kate consoles herself, it is she who has departed. All this internal turmoil, yet she is merely caught up in the commonplace practice of moving from one room into another. The room of being a mother of an adolescent into that of being a mother of a woman who is herself a mother now. These are different situations requiring different strategies.

There will be other rooms in the future.

The child and the sketchbook are silent. The piano

is silent. The berg outside the kitchen window does not protest.

The girl picks at the cultivated, cultured curd, swinging her legs under the table with stifled longing.

Kate recalls the evening when her own mother, the long-suffering Mother Mary, sat in the same chair where Kate sits now. She insisted that Jessica could not leave the table until she finished her meal. Good food. Food made the hard way, by means of her grandmother's hands. Yet Kate could see that the resentment in her mother's body had passed through her hands and entered the food, simmering beneath Jess's gaze. She'd refused to eat it, intuitively not wanting to taint her young life with her grandmother's anxieties, her own pure anger blooming in her cheeks.

Kate had wanted Jessica to win. Those days when she was not the target of her daughter's intransigence, she was secretly proud of her. Jessica had sat it out for two hours. Then the cottage pie, or whatever it was, suddenly disappeared off her plate. Her grandmother, worn down, accepted that Jessica had eaten it, although they all knew she had slipped it to the dogs.

Jessica has fed me to the dogs, thinks Kate.

Life, she muses, is a succession of rooms through

which we move at varying speeds and with varying degrees of volition. There are even doors you can fall through, trapdoors that give way, so you arrive in strange circumstances without warning, no turning back. Like falling pregnant, and motherhood.

Kate, or Jess, could have had an abortion. They could have avoided all this. They could have chosen other lives, other men, other sets of difficulties.

Get the brandy from the cupboard, she tells herself, stir a generous dash into the cream while waiting for the pans to heat.

Leonard was the man she had chosen, the one who, ten years into marriage at a Valentine's Day dinner, proclaimed that he had always loved to 'sample the essences' of many women, but now chose not to do so for love of his wife. This while he was fucking someone else, one of a gaggle of ogle-eyed fans.

The two pans are hot enough. Pour in dollops of batter, tilt the pans so that it runs into thin yellow discs, covering the bases.

Kate lifts the lid of another large pot on the stove and dips a teaspoon in to sample the contents. Pap without salt for the initiates. Nosisi and the other mothers cook food for their sons during this time although they may not set eyes upon them.

Kate smiles at the thought of serving this bland food to the Frenchmen in order to make men of them.

There is the unsolved question of how to turn a boy into a man, one that can be true and who does not resort to violence or secret lives like a schoolboy hiding his naughtiness from his mother. She wonders how Leonard lives with his deceit. After all these years, these questions still ache in Kate's side.

Sex addiction, her doctor explained, as she treated Kate for chlamydia, is under-diagnosed. She understands that Leonard has an illness – the obsessive compulsion to grapple yet another vulnerable student or fan club reader into bed.

Flip the pancakes. One. Then the other.

Both ready, and onto the plate, Nosisi adds the sauce, the marinated pears and a garnish of mint leaves. More butter into the pans, sizzling, then another two rounds of batter. Adjust the heat.

Leonard will always be part of Kate's life. Their daughter was the product of their conjoining, when she opened her trust and body and future to this man. Jess was created during those early days, when they disturbed and excited each other with the respite of sex. Kate had imagined she was receiving life.

Things were clearer in her great-grandmother's day, she decides. Women knew that making love carried a terrible risk. Sex could make babies. Having babies could kill the mother – ruptured wombs, bleeding to death, infection. There are remedies for those problems now. Other difficulties have emerged. Now HIV can insert itself. Lie with your body, and your deceit can murder.

The Frenchmen are laughing uproariously. Their humour has been restored.

Tanya's mother is saying that the country is going to the dogs and that any white person in their right mind should emigrate.

Where to? Kate wants to drop the smiling hostess mask and shove this question at her guest. The problems, she wants to emphasise, are global. Corruption in a black man is seen as base, whereas corruption in a white man is associated with sophistication. Why is this?

The sketchbook-snatcher looks up as Kate places dessert before her. Aren't you afraid, she asks. Living here on your own?

I am neither afraid nor am I on my own, Kate wants

to exclaim. I have never, and I mean *never*, been hurt by a black man, but white men have hurt me frequently.

There is a risk, living here. Farmers have been attacked and murdered in this country. Ordinary thugs have done this, also those who wish to retaliate against white people who stole land that used to belong to everyone and to no one, land that used to produce food for all.

Down the ages those in power have laid exclusive claim, Kate knows, they have subjugated the land, tamed and portioned her off. They have fenced her and controlled her. Enslaved her, force-fed her with chemicals so that she produces more and more. The same strategy is used with cows – injecting hormones in order to extract more milk than the body would naturally produce.

Kate wants to explain: We live off the body of our mother, the earth, and we take and take, and waste and bloat, then cut off the breast that feeds us.

The girl's mother is still looking at her, awaiting her reply.

Yes, Kate wants to respond, I am afraid. Afraid of what humans have done in the name of progress. I am afraid that we are so alienated from our animal bodies and the earth that we are killing ourselves, taking all life with us.

Instead she says to the snatcher, reassuringly: I have dogs. And good people who work with me.

The woman glowers up at her in disbelief, wanting Kate to affirm her version and vision of the world, wanting Kate to yoke her ideas to hers so that they can both pull in the same direction. But Kate continues: I love this place. I will do what it takes to remain here.

The whole table is looking at Kate. She wants Tanya to hear something different from what she has been brought up to believe, so she continues: I have received so much from living here that I want to participate in making this country a better place.

These are just words, she berates herself. I should offer to teach Elihle to make cheese, or to drive. She pushes on, wanting to hear her own words: I will stay in this country unless there is gross abuse, unless that abuse is so intolerable that I am forced to leave. Being a citizen is a marriage of sorts.

Kate knows herself to be a committed person. Tanya's mother needs to know that she did not leave her husband easily.

Oom Fanie is opening his mouth, ready to object,

so Kate quickly inserts: Have to see to the other table, excuse me, and leaves Fanie and his family to argue the point.

Although she has the urge to turn back and remind Fanie's family that white women of her generation in this country are one of the few groups in the history of the world that have not had to deal directly with overt war in their lifetime. It is rare to get off that lightly. Revolutionary change was never going to be easy. The damaged past still resides within us, shoved under our hope, tripping us up.

From the emotional abuse she experienced during her marriage, she understands the impulse towards revenge that resides in the hearts of those who have been hurt. Particularly when the hurt goes unacknowledged by the perpetrator. Kate knows, it is not possible to make amends when you don't recognise a violation in all its consequences.

Merci. The balding Frenchman nods his appreciation as Kate places the dessert in front of him.

Jessica has left this magnificent, difficult land, and she has left her mother, a double betrayal. Her daughter claims she does not miss her mother country, but Kate cannot believe her.

Kate returns to the kitchen, refills the kettle.

No! she hears, behind her. She turns to see Nosisi holding her hand up in front of her averted face as a flash illuminates the room. Greybeard has followed Kate into the kitchen and is pointing his camera at Nosisi. I said, no! Nosisi's trembling voice repeats.

Greybeard lowers his camera. No photo? He asks, sounding hurt, a little boy.

Nosisi turns away and wipes the kitchen counter with vigour. You are a visitor here, she points out.

Not very welcome, Greybeard says. His mood has changed from bewilderment to annoyance. He replaces the cap on the camera lens.

You are not used to the tourist here, he says. This is, what do you call it? The backwater.

You take without permission, Nosisi snaps. She has often posed at the request of guests. Gert rouses her anger, and she sometimes shouts at Luzoko, but Kate has never seen her react like this to a stranger.

Please, Kate interjects, ushering Greybeard back

out towards the stoep. We do not allow guests in the kitchen.

A lie, but necessary under the circumstances.

Bien sûr, we are in any case going.

Qu'est-ce que c'est? The young man puts his dessert spoon down and dabs at his mouth with his serviette.

C'est rien. Greybeard looks at his watch and reaches into his jacket pocket for his wallet.

Kate writes the receipt and exchanges it for his money. She needs them to leave before there are any more upheavals.

As the three foreigners drive away, Kate wants to laugh, thinking about Greybeard's shock and indignation at being refused by a woman, and a black one at that.

Although it also isn't funny. Nosisi is offended. The restaurant has a reputation to uphold in the face of rude customers. And Kate is sliding around in the imbalances between paying guest, restaurant owner and employee. These watershed moments – when to acquiesce and when to object.

Nosisi needs to go home now, it is her birthday, and they are both tired and fragile today.

There is the order for the deli to prepare. Kate goes

inside and approaches the remaining party: Oom Fanie, is it still alright for you to take the cheese order through to Lucas's?

Ja. He looks at his watch. But soon, we must be op pad. After coffee.

Two forty-seven. Twelve forty-seven over there. Six hours into the surgery and no word. No time to phone, to do the right thing. Busyness is an antidote to everything.

Kate grabs a ripe pear from the kitchen. She wants to say something about the awkward encounter, but Nosisi is grinding the coffee beans, her body turned away from any attempt at conversation. So Kate walks across the field to the cellar underneath the cheese room to fetch the order for Oom Fanie to drop off at the farm stall as arranged, saving her a trip. She bites into the pear and her mouth is filled with juice and delicate flavour. This fruit is such a relief, she thinks, but from what? Boarding school, with its overcooked food. She still has a limb in the trap of her childhood, even as she eats this pear. One leg in the encumbrance of the sterile years she endured at boarding school, the other in the Leonard trap, despite coming all the way to the countryside in an attempt to release herself.

An uncomfortable twinge in her belly. Squatting down out of sight behind the shed, she relaxes her faithful bladder which empties itself, the warm fluid spurting a tiny depression into the earth, then running down the slope and soaking away. A dark wet crust of soil. Rorschach: an amoeba pointing downhill with one long tentacle.

The spider, at her elbow, has reconstructed the web. Kate observes how accurately she has measured the spaces between the cross-strands. There is so much to be amazed by every day in the natural world. The spider crouches on a twig of the bush, one of the supports for her elegant net, and waits with a leg hooked under a strand like a fisherwoman with a finger under her line waiting to apprehend the slightest tug.

Kate rises, pulling her jeans back up. At the dam's edge she rinses her hands. The water is a pleasant temperature and there is a prickle of sweat at the base of her spine. She will find time to swim today, she vows. Ridiculous how she is still rushing, running away from the terror of sitting with nothing to do, her hands lying orphaned in her lap. What would they do if left to their own devices without the directives of the brain and the restraint of social demands?

Her hands, two old servants, wet from immersion. They are becoming her mother's hands. Bangles of wrinkles are gathering at her wrists. Her fingers spread themselves under her gaze, awaiting instruction. Extraordinary instruments, capable of tenderness and violence, creativity and destruction; willing tools, ready to embark on innumerable tasks at her bidding. They have served her well. They long to sing the language of the piano with their ten willing tongues.

Not now! the executive officer of the brain decrees, and most sensibly. There is cheese to be wrapped. Kate opens the heavy, insulated door and enters the dark musk of the cellar. The fridge motor starts up as her intrusion introduces the heat of the day. Switching the light on, she finds the tray marked on the day they were made: *5 Nov*. Forty silken white pyramid cheeses. Absolute perfection.

This cellar emulates the caves where cheeses were left in the old days to develop their flavour through the action of bacteria, mould and fungus. Humans harnessing the invisible world to a visible end. Nowadays, there is a terror of what can't be seen, and anti-bacterial soaps and preservatives are commonplace. Kate recalls how, when she started her first job as a tutor at the university, she had to cancel her first microbiology prac owing to the fact that the bread she'd bought hadn't grown fungus because of the added preservatives. The students had nothing to study, and Kate decided never to eat non-artisanal bread again.

At Lucas's farm stall, her cheeses will all sell by the end of the day. This is a worthy life if excellence in cheese makes the world a better place. If the daily making of cheese by hand is a proper job. Yet thirty percent of purchased food is thrown away, frets Kate. If it's true of her produce, that's thirteen cheeses made with love and care that are discarded without a thought. Waste in a world of famine. The poor looking through rubbish bins for something to eat is a central image of our times.

Nosisi sees Kate coming and opens the door. Kate goes through to the kitchen and places the tray on the table. Oom Fanie has paid the bill and is hovering, wanting to go. Ek kom nou, Oom, she tells him.

The two women wrap each cheese and place them carefully in an insulated box. Kate gives Oom Fanie an elegant cheese from the fridge as payment for his trouble. He is pleased, but his girlfriend's face works through a range of emotions as he hands it to her. The woman is disgusted by the mould. Her plate on the sideboard has all suspect cheese cut away and scraped to one side.

Oom Fanie leans his face forward to stick a wet and prickly kiss onto Kate's cheek.

While ushering them out, Kate tries to catch Tanya's eye, wishing to indicate that her liaison with her grandfather is of necessity, but that she is on Tanya's side. The girl has her drawing book tucked protectively under her arm and the pencil case in her hand. She can't wait to get home, to try to catch again the loose end of the line and follow it down into the unknown.

Kate puts a hand on the girl's shoulder as encouragement, but she breaks away and runs for the van. Kate is left standing amongst chickens and dogs as the family gets in, waving and slamming doors. They drive away, taking elements of this land with them. The food derived from the living earth of this district is even now, as their van disappears through the trees lining the driveway, being dissembled inside their bodies, only to be reassembled into their bodies. The iron in the green of spinach turning into the red of their blood, the protein incorporated into muscle, the fatty acids in the cheese metamorphosing into neural tissue. She hopes her produce will feed the girl's ability to think and feel for herself, straight and well.

Nosisi is in the scullery, washing up. That man! Kate exclaims. We should put up a sign on the door saying shut up and sit down. Her employee makes a sound of dissatisfaction in her throat. Go home early Sisi, it's your birthday.

Again, the grunt of annoyance.

Sisi? You know how customers can be.

He has the photographs.

Oh, these tourists snap away all the time, he'll hardly look at them again.

He took without asking.

Well, there's not much we can do now.

You have his phone number.

Yes, he did the booking.

He must delete. The ones of me. And Luzoko.

Oh-kay. Fat chance he'll listen.

Nosisi stops washing the dishes and turns, gesturing down the length of her body, water dripping off her hands. This is mine. Mine! she says, confronting Kate. You said nothing.

Kate opens her mouth, wanting to defend herself and protest the point. This issue, amongst all those that press down on women, on black women, is hardly the one to take up as a cause, surely. But there is something in the way Nosisi is standing, holding herself, her legs planted, her chest open yet defiant. Her employee's body has worked on the farm for over thirty years, baking cakes for family members on their birthdays, welcoming her home from boarding school with pumpkin fritters and golden syrup, attending Kate's wedding here on the farm dressed in traditional Shweshwe clothing with head scarf. This faithful body that used to pick up baby Jessica and swing her onto her back to press against her warmth, tied with a blanket while she did her chores, that made sure girl Jess washed before lunch, holding her small grubby hands under running water, that has scrubbed the floors and cleaned the bath and cooked thousands of meals for first her parents and now herself, carrying buckets of water and bags of potatoes, that has washed Kate's clothes and tidied her cupboards, that patiently fed her mother mashed banana and milk when she was too weak to feed herself. The beloved body that sobbed in Kate's arms when her own daughter died, the body that became tense with acceptance when Luzoko left, and that lives with her aunt in a tiny house on a small plot in the township at the foot of the mountain. The body that has acquiesced and conformed to so much, has borne so much. That body now refuses.

Kate fetches the handset and looks up the number on the restaurant booking sheet.

It's easier to phone France than England, she consoles herself. Nevertheless, she is relieved when France answers as a recorded message in Greybeard's voice and mother tongue, presumably telling her to leave a message: This is Kate Newman, your host at lunch. There is a problem you need to correct, please. The photographs of my helper, Nosisi, and her son, one of the young men by the river – delete them. Thank you.

She switches off. Nosisi is standing with her arms folded and shoulders hunched, staring out of the window above the sink towards the berg. There are so many mistakes in the world that are difficult to put right. Oh Sisi, Kate says, we should have got Gert to make that call. She drops her voice, adopting gravel notes: Fok Meneer, wipe those blerry photos off your phone onmiddellik or I'll donner you.

Nosisi is silent, then she chuckles. Fok Meneer! she laughs. Next time I'll tell him, Fok Meneer!

Fok them all, I need some lunch. Kate opens the fridge to peruse the possibilities. There is a bowl of bean salad and some leftover bread on the table.

One day, Sisi, when black women are in charge, I hope you'll forgive us, she says, putting the food and handset on a tray. Go home, I'll finish up.

The Frenchmen have left half a glass of wine on their table outside which would be a shame to waste. She sits and wolfs down the salad with a spoon. A good bean salad, just the right proportions of vinegar and honey, oil, herbs and seasoning. Sips the wine. It will fortify her for the next task. Tasks, stacking up. A moment to rest, looking out over her farm, sipping the delicious wine.

Nosisi's comment: taking without permission. All of this, the land. The original made-up title deeds cannot so easily be deleted. The crimes of Kate's ancestors have ensured that she lives this life of relative luxury. She has had choices and the resources to change her circumstances when she'd had enough.

It's three o'clock. Back in the city, at three on a

Wednesday afternoon, Kate would have been handing a pipette containing fertilised, incubated, cultured, DNA-checked, perfect embryos through the hatch to the theatre sister in the operating room beyond. The infertility specialist, gloved and gowned, would be positioned between the spread and stirrupped legs of a reclining, draped and hopeful woman, pressing his ultrasound probe onto her lower abdomen and looking at an image of her reproductive innards on a screen. With a speculum, he would open her vagina, then guide the end of the pipette through the opening of the cervix. Carefully, he would insert the embryos into her uterus, three in all. A man working away between a woman's legs. Men at work.

Years later, successful mothers sometimes brought their children to see the lab. This is where you were made, they would declare, scarcely believing it themselves. They would then turn with adulation towards the beaming specialist: Thank you so very, very much, Doctor!

Thought made flesh. The little brat that was once a few cells in Kate's culture would run around the office, not listening to his mother.

There were those who could not conceive no matter

what they tried. One desperate woman pressed a gift into Kate's palm and asked her to pray over her darling dividing zygote to improve the chances of success.

Women are either weeping because they are not pregnant, or because they are, Kate muses. She and Jess both fell pregnant despite themselves. She wonders whether her daughter wept when the test came up positive, as she did.

Nosisi comes outside, and glances at the glass of wine, underlining that she has noticed that Kate has taken to polishing off the dregs at lunchtime once the guests had gone.

Would you like a glass, for your birthday?

No. Of course, Nosisi doesn't drink. She hands Kate the receipts and takings. A hundred rand a head times nine is nine hundred plus two hundred in tips and nearly six hundred for the drinks.

The quiche is in the oven, Nosisi says, untying her apron. Turn it on before supper.

Thank you. Kate hands her another hundred to make them both feel better.

That rude one is a boy still.

Yep, blame the fact that we don't have initiation rituals. Drugs and motorbikes are the closest our boys get. You need a lift?

Mr Wilhelm is taking me. Kate's neighbour, who is building a house for one of his labourers in the township. Before you leave, Nosisi says, meaning London, we need flour, also onions.

You'll be okay?

You must go. Daughters are not like sons.

And if another Frenchman is rude to you?

Nosisi lifts her chin. I can defend myself.

There goes my business, Kate frets to herself.

It's not so difficult to run this place, Nosisi tells her. Go. She picks up Kate's empty bowl and the wine bottle. I'm praying for you all, she says and goes through to the kitchen. Kate hears the sound of the front door closing.

At last, Kate is alone. A consternation starts up in her chest. She doesn't want to be on her own after all.

A quarter past three. There is some wine left in the bottom of Oom Fanie's second bottle. She drinks it straight, sucking at the mouth of the bottle. Suck,

suck, suck, drinking too fast. The warm flush eases the clutch, it takes the edge off. Slight swirl in her head. She sits surveying her land, facing north over the dam to the berg. Over the berg is London, the locus of hurt heads.

This is what she wants to say to her daughter: I wanted a baby, Jessica, unlike your father who only fell in love with you around the time you turned two. At last, I thought, seeing his pleasure when he started reading books with you. At last he could love you.

She had hoped that having a child would wake something in Leonard. Perhaps now, she'd thought, he will love me too.

Bloody nice wine, she savours. I have a mind to open another.

No, Kate. Time for the piano, a different intoxication. She stands, steadies herself. Then goes inside and sits down at the piano with a flourish, as though about to perform in a concert hall.

'La répétition', the French word for practice, her mother's reminder. Start with the D major scale.

She focuses: My fingers, lying over the keys, depressing my fingertips, starting to work my way over the keyboard, work, not fly, as my hands should.

Start again, god, that was terrible, my hands cold and stiff, my fingering wrong. Notes falling into the room. And again, it's coming back, the thumb going under, third finger, thumb under, left hand weak, too weak, lead with the left to force it to work harder, my hands perhaps kept in some kind of shape by the exercise of milking goats, now milking these notes out of my mother's instrument, and back, and here we go, damn, start again. Leonard's voice in my head – I haven't heard that noise since I was at school – damn him. Again, I *will* get this right. My hands will remember.

This room itself remembers these notes hammered out by all three of her mother's daughters. Start again. Up and down; up and down. Now contrary motion, till the blood starts flowing to the fingertips, fingertips flowing over the keys. Turn effortful into effortless, the way of enlightenment. La répétition, répétition, until she breaks through what Gilbert called 'the sound barrier', that shift from being outside the music, start again, to finding herself inside the cathedral of sound, the body aligned, forgotten, and again, working away at the surface resistance, the interface between mind and body, body and instrument, instrument and the gods, her fingers trying to prise open the lid she has so firmly shut on her capabilities, trying to sing it open, start again, and again, hands not quite in sync, left hand trailing, E minor melodic scale, shoulders tight, relax Kate, into the patterned movement, intention firing neurons stirring fingers striking keys striking strings trying to get the air in the room to sing, too much effort, smaller movements, damn, again, again, répétition, practice, practice, without which she will always remain outside the most sacred realm, not called the harmony of the spheres for nothing.

Breathe.

C major, only the ivories, damn, terrible, start again, and again. Again. Her mind clamps to this task like a Rottweiler, start again, damn, don't end on the wrong finger, how did that happen, again, and again, try to transform this army drill into a transcendent meditation, how to clear her head, restring her body, again, now a D major arpeggio, legato, it's coming, again, that was almost perfect, the pleasure of success interrupting, and there she goes again, pinkie won't operate properly, always some lazy bugger on the team, at least there's no one to hear her; again. Again.

Again. Her hands released, two birds in flight.

Again. Choices of volume, tempo, phrasing, and

feeling made with every note, with every second of each living day.

Again. Better.

She glances at the clock. Three forty-six. Surprised to find she has been at this for half an hour. Music alters the usual progression. Time becomes space.

One can never be sufficiently prepared. Kate opens the sheet music at random. Chopin's Raindrop Prelude. She used to be able to play this and can surely learn it again, the pathways still lying around old and mouldy in the brain. They just need to be given a good shake-out, or an oiling.

She used to play this piece of music as though she was dreaming. The genius of Chopin, creating poetic spaces for humans to inhabit, opening consummate beauty.

Her fingers are lying lightly on the keyboard. The piano waits, willing, offering its silent chords up into her hands. Kate watched a visiting musician playing the cello at a recent recital in the village, how the fine-tuned instrument of his body engaged and communed with the cello; how they became one, like lovers, out of which rose the miracle of Bach's Cello suite in C major. Once again, Kate saw how her earlier attempts to play the piano had had the wrong emphasis or attitude, how she had approached the piano as though to extract music from a dead mechanism, as if mining for minerals. She watched him play, the music opening a portal onto an Eden she feared will never be within her reach.

Afraid, too, that the same attitude has formed and informed her life for too long – instead of interchange and exchange, she has approached life as a lifeless entity to be subdued, conquered or endured. Or be defeated by.

Kate depresses her fingers in the prescribed combinations illustrated on the page in front of her, and is carried into the opening bars of Chopin, the sound releasing in lumps and whimpers, filling her with despair. Expectations thwarted, yet like an obstinate, trusting, kicked dog, she is back for more, trying again. Her mother stands at her shoulder looking on with a cold eye. Kate's life, her ideals have fallen away, and yet she keeps attempting to glue some pieces back together, pieces that no longer contain or fit her shape.

Try again. She tries to quieten her mind so that music can enter. Again. There are hesitations, errors.

Her fingers will not obey, they are stiff and stupid. Patience, Kate. Start again.

Wrong handful of notes. Start again.

But how many times can one start again when life is looking so much shorter? When she was young, she did not understand that life is lived between brackets. Now she sees, here comes the end bracket. The terror of discovering that you still do not know what you were born for.

Her mother Mary was a miner of the piano. She might have had moments of rapture inside the gold seam. You will get out of this what you put into it, her mother's words admonish her. Not so hard Kate! This is not a concerto!

Wrong fingering; start again.

Mother Mary said: Learning the piano is like going on a journey. If you are only thinking about the destination, it spoils the journey.

Start again.

Again.

Kate crashes her fists down on the keys, setting the dogs off. There is no going back. She can no longer please her mother and thereby please herself. She can no longer please Leonard, nor Jessica.

Kate rises and puts on Evgeny Kissin's rendition of the Raindrop Prelude and throws herself onto the sofa. Caesar approaches, places his great consoling head in her lap. Her hand falls onto the animal's back to stroke him while the maestro creates great beauty.

How would it be if music were to leave my life? she wonders. If she woke up one day without the beginnings of some composition in her head. Or if she sold the piano to prevent it from staring at her. Losing the piano, losing music would be like losing the beauty and tyranny of her mother, the hard task master presiding over that elusive state of grace. Merging of the musician with the music. A blessing and a curse that still calls.

The tension held by the musical raindrops hints at the approaching storm. Caesar's breath is hot on her hand, Brutus noses in jealously. The cushion presses behind her back, her head rests in the hot block of sun descending through the window and onto the sofa's backrest. Kate's two dogs are attendant, waiting, their tails whipping the air.

Outside, there is living water in the dam, so different from the dead fluid she used to swim through in the pool at the city gym, rendered lifeless by chlorine.

As the storm in the music strikes, marking the end of one melody and the beginning of another, Kate stands. She must immerse herself. She turns up the volume as high as it can go and walks out onto the stoep as the piece reaches the crescendo, the dogs winding excitedly around her. Music to drown by, it occurs to her. The perfect dramatic score.

She walks down the path to the trees at the edge of the dam, Chopin trailing, suffusing the air. The dogs bound into the water, their great paws generating splashes and clouds of turbulence.

Kate pulls her shirt over her head, kicks off her boots and pulls her jeans down. The Leisure Consorts are nowhere to be seen, but even if they were, she would swim naked. There is an African tradition where, if women are incensed, they take off their clothes as a gesture of protest. Here, Kate reasons, where there has been a failure of both the law and common decency to prevent the golf estate travesty, she will resort to an ancient method. She will shake her furious breasts, she will show them her outraged buttocks.

On reflection, things could have got way more interesting when Nosisi confronted Greybeard.

She forgot to make Nosisi Crêpes Suzette.

The water slips over her skin like silk. Diving under, she wonders why she resists this amniotic pleasure, this weightless, tender holding.

Following the dogs, she strikes out for the island in the middle of the dam, the one she and Jess used to row to and picnic on when she was little. The piece of driftwood her daughter found there and adorned with strings of beads and feathers and seeds then hung up in her room. She always had an eye for things of beauty.

Her intelligent, artistic daughter had worked as an assistant on set, making people pretty for commercials. It's the one place where creativity is rewarded, Jess had argued. I mean, have you even seen the BMW ad, or the Revlon one? You don't even have a TV, you don't know what you are talking about! These ads are works of art. You're so critical, but look at you. Providing luxuries for rich men with big bellies.

Daniel says there is no longer such a thing as a luxury amongst the middle classes. If there is any food one hankers for, one can easily get it down at the local deli, flown in from a source anywhere in the world.

All this in a time of food shortages. Abundance amidst famine.

If the phone rings, Kate won't hear it above the music, never get to it in time, so she heads back towards the rich strains of the Brahms Intermezzo in A major, doing breast stroke with her head up so as to hear the music flooding over the surface of the water.

The gathering of trees at the dam's edge has multiplied since she was a child, sending out their seedlings. She has read that six million trees are harvested every month in the USA for mail-order catalogues alone.

Kate wades out of the water, heading for the cover of the trees. Pulls her clothes on, against the cloying wetness of her skin. The dogs are ferreting in the undergrowth, chasing some small terrified animal, their tails winding like handles. She calls them off, promising them mass-produced chunks that lie boringly in their bowls, thinking that some dog food manufacturer should produce dog food that runs around and has to be caught for extra canine gastronomic satisfaction.

Kate bends, and shakes out her hair, the sunlight catching strands. The Cheddar. Time for another turn of the screw. Down the path to the cheese room.

Open the door. Turn the wheel, compressing

the truckle further, yielding small trickles of whey through the pores of the mould.

Four twenty-three. Time for coffee. How much longer do I have to myself, she wonders, not wanting to milk the goats. This time alone is too precious.

Back to the house along the path that is a single thread in the vast web of roads and highways and paths, that holds the whole world in its net.

Through to the kitchen with the Brahms Intermezzo coming to an end, wet dogs trailing.

Silence, but for the buzz of a fly on glass. Kate opens the window to let it out, trying for silence. She is in need of vast deserts of silence. Switch the kettle on, open the fridge to fetch coffee and milk. A bottle of cleaning liquid is on the second shelf next to the yoghurt. Slipped past Elihle's monitoring eye. No wonder Kate can never find anything. Yesterday, the basin was full of strands of toilet paper.

A pricking of Kate's skin tells her: There is someone else in the room. She swings round, her heart thumping. A man, standing not two metres away.

My god, she breathes, here is the man I loved for many years. Standing in my kitchen. He has just walked into my life as though he is still part of it. As though it was the days when Mum was alive and Da understood how to use a toothbrush, and they lived here together and we were visiting on holiday with our daughter. As though Jess, any moment now, would come running in on her thin young legs with a jar full of tadpoles, exclaiming.

Leonard has not aged well with his wispy grey hair, his paunch, his sallow nicotine skin, yet he still emanates his hallmark boyish charm that women seem to find irresistible.

Why didn't I hear him arrive? she wonders. It was the music.

She worries that he might have seen her naked. Rakes her wet hair back with her fingers.

So he is not yet in London.

As Leonard comes towards her and bends to kiss her on the lips, she veers, turning her cheek into a shield, feeling the wet of his lip, the lip that has fed on the desire of so many women.

Can I come in? Leonard asks, smiling.

Kate ignores this nonsense. She gestures tiredly to a

chair. Coffee or tea? she offers.

He looks around critically, his familiar gesture. Coffee, please.

What brings you out here?

Business, over the berg, so I thought I'd pop in.

There is no obvious function to his lying now. She speculates that he has a story about who he is, and that everything has to support that story. There's a faint disc of light behind his head. Some believe such manifestations to be auras but Kate understands that they are the constructed story that must be held intact at any cost.

I've got to milk the goats soon, she warns. Gert's afternoon off.

She also has her aura story. They can sit and be nice to each other for a short while, she supposes, each contained by a halo light.

Kate realises that he is waiting for her to ask. It's a slow turning of the screw. He is watching her as she pushes the coffee plunger down with more force than necessary and pours the dark liquid into Sharon's mugs.

Milk? Sugar? She is pleased she doesn't remember this domestic detail, which is surely a sign that this man is receding at last from her life.

Black, please.

Kate gives him the mug and sits down with the broad kitchen table between them. His blue eyes are on her, waiting, then they wander down to her breasts, appraising her ageing. He offers a smile like a handout to the poor: You look like Old McDonald.

Kate smiles rigidly back, pretending this is only a joke. And succumbs, before her brain can stop her. Has Jessica –?

He lifts one eyebrow ever so slightly: You could've phoned by now –

Sharon's voice plays sternly in Kate's head: Don't pick up the rope. Summoning enormous effort, she stops herself from reacting angrily.

Don't pick up the rope. Don't pick up the rope.

It takes two to play tug of war, she reminds herself. In a tug of war only one can win.

Leonard takes a sip of coffee, then produces a pouch of roll-up tobacco from his shoulder bag, a film canister and some Rizlas. I have been in contact with her every half hour. The aureole behind his head flares briefly, noticeably. He looks at his watch. It could take another two, maybe three hours – he stops mid-sentence and leans forward, bringing his cupped right hand slowly into view, focussing on a fly settled on the table top that is rubbing its stubby legs – before we know. With a quick, deft movement, he sweeps his hand across the table and holds his closed fist up triumphantly before dashing the fly to the floor. His old party trick.

That was me, Kate thinks.

So, Storm and Sky are still alive, she breathes. They are still holding on by a thread to life and to each other. In a white room full of masked adults leaning over them, swathed in strange green garb and manipulating instruments.

He taps some dope out into his palm, glances over at Kate: Want some?

She shakes her head. Leonard snaps the canister closed and rolls the joint. He gestures towards the stoep. Kate follows him outside, the old, familiar pattern. Leonard sits, scans the lake, puts the end of the joint between his lips, lights up and pulls relief into his chest through the cerise tip. He tilts his head back on the hinge of his neck and exhales a long trumpet of grey. Kate remembers this gesture. Again she catches herself looking at this man who was usually looking somewhere else.

She sits down across from him, her legs restless. I thought you had already flown over.

Jessica asked me to come tomorrow. He coughs. Inhales again.

Maybe it's better they don't make it. Terrible start to a life. There, she has said it.

Leonard regards Kate, taking his time. Worse things have happened, he says.

Yes, she agrees. Much worse.

Beethoven's Ninth, vibrating in electronic mode. Leonard leans back in his chair and wrestles his cellphone out of his jeans pocket. Jessica, Kate hopes, steeling herself.

He applies the phone to his ear. Hello? Leonard Rycroft here. His telephone voice.

Leonard Rycroft. The famous Leonard Rycroft is sitting stoned on her stoep.

Years back, some svelte woman rushed up to Kate at a party. You are so lucky to be married to Leonard Rycroft! she exclaimed, excited and gleaming. This was the week after Kate had found out about his third affair. She grinned at the woman bleakly, excused herself, faltered down the passage and bolted herself into the toilet, weeping.

Yes, this is the author. A pause, while Leonard focuses. I am the grandfather. He leans forward, interested. He nods. All right. Yes. No. We don't know yet. They are still in the theatre.

The theatre. Kate understands: Her grandsons are performing for the media. People have always loved a freak show.

Leonard has adopted his dramatic face: Yes, very unusual. Fifty-fifty chance, they say. He takes a last drag, presses the stub out on the heel of his shoe, throws it into her garden. This was one of the marital wars she never won. Even divorce cannot prevent him from coming round to litter her life with the discarded stubs of his pleasure.

Of course. In about two hours. We should know by then. He nods. It's a pleasure, Joanne, it was Joanne? Phone me later. He switches off, puts the phone on the table between them. It idles there, waiting. He drinks the last of his coffee. That was the *Guardian*. This is an international event.

I wouldn't speak to the papers if I were you.

Leonard frowns. Why ever not? People have a right to know. It could happen to anyone. We have a duty to help others cope with tragedy. Otherwise what is the use of going through this trauma ourselves? Irritation sits in the slant of his shoulders, the tap of his fingers, the reflex reach for his cigarettes in his shirt pocket. It's not as though this is the *Sun*, or *You* magazine.

Kate cannot help thinking that publicity of any kind is good for an author.

If we don't release the correct story, they are bound to publish something inaccurate, Leonard continues.

Maybe I am a bitch. Maybe he cares, deeply.

He lights up, drags hard, then leans towards Kate and takes her hand. She feels life drain out of it. Her hand becomes a limp object in his grip. She remembers his caress. And she is in need of being held.

What have we done, Kate?

We? She is taken aback. Leonard's soft eyes are upon her, pleading: You are the love of my life.

The table is in the way. Thank god she put the table between them, the pull is so strong. Like a black hole invitation to merge, to let this all go, the hard life alone. Leonard reaches into his bag with his other hand, not letting her go. Pulls out a white envelope. Places it with emphasis on the table in front of her.

The real reason I came, he begins – Kate's whole body is on alert – was to tell you I have booked you a ticket on the three forty-five plane tomorrow. Come to London with me, Kate. Jess could do with both her parents. We must stand together through this.

A twist of relief and grief tightens in her.

Leonard touches her cheek, tenderly. I have booked us into a B&B near the hospital. Separate rooms.

A yearning ignited by his fingers touching her face connects to her sex, which is flowering open against the hardness of the chair. The table edge digs its restraint into her belly, reminding her.

I can't leave at the moment. Maybe next week.

She withdraws her hand.

Leonard stands, comes round to her side of the table, takes her hands and pulls her up out of her chair. She acquiesces, but there is something wrong with her leg bones, or her knees. Something is again attacking the mechanism by which she holds herself upright in the world. Leonard gathers her up and holds her against his chest.

We'll pay Gert extra, he'll keep things going. And Nosisi and that boy who looks after your Dad. Your daughter needs you. His voice cracks. I need you.

He strokes Kate's hair like a lover would. She is filled with an urge to take him into her mouth and suck, to suck and suck. So hungry. Starving amidst plenty.

And pulls away, with huge effort, shaken, shaking. Trying to recover herself in her own skin. I must see to something, Kate mutters. And turns. Away.

She finds herself in the kitchen, her body aching. It is so hard to know what is going on, stumbling around in her mind. Looking around the room. Searching. She is here for a reason but cannot remember.

Reaches for the coffee urn. Perhaps there is a way, she fumbles. Poor man. It must be terrible to be caught in a sexual compulsion. Driving the one person you love away ...

Perhaps he has changed, she considers. She does believe in change. Perhaps this tragedy is the very thing that could bring them together.

She could go over with him. Jess would welcome them both with relief. If Kate forgives Leonard, her daughter will forgive her. The twins will be healed and all will be well. Kate can cancel the second room at the B&B and receive this man, make him her husband again, take him to her so that they can all be consoled. He would repent in her arms, weeping, forsake all other women, and she would forgive him all his transgressions. They would be delivered, and the mandala of the family restored. The circle of life revived, revitalised.

Through the window, Kate sees his car. There is someone sitting in Leonard's car. There is someone in Leonard's car, in the passenger seat, waiting. A woman. She can see a woman sitting and waiting in Leonard's car. She cannot believe what she is seeing.

Believe it, Kate. This fact smacks her cold.

This is life come round again, right on cue, she reminds her shocked self. Life is gently pointing something out, again, my darling. In case you still haven't got it.

In her driveway there sits yet another woman who is familiar with Leonard's intimate gestures.

Another, who sits like a dog chained to a pole, waiting for its master to return.

I could go out there and untie her, invite her in, Kate fumes. Or I could go outside, and order her to get off my property. I could smack her through the face – how dare she? What on earth is she doing here, now, today? I could go out, slip into the driver's seat, and interview her about her situation. I could even, kindly, offer some advice.

Mistresses never take the time to get the back story.

The woman is not the problem, it occurs to her. The woman. Is not. The problem.

Pathetic creature. Kate recognises her. There was a time she would sit quietly in the car of Leonard's life and do what she was told.

The woman, she acknowledges, is also the problem.

She has a soft profile, Kate notes, studying what she can see of her while trying not to be seen. Or sad, perhaps. She is young. Naïve. What has she been told? That Kate is the possessive ex-wife, the harridan, the Gorgon? What has restrained this car woman so effectively? The story of twins, operations, disaster? Leonard has been here for over half an hour.

Kate's body is in flames.

I will keep him here, she decides. I will prolong his stay. I will find her out.

Wine, she schemes. I will present him with good wine, even though it is not yet five. That will delay him. He will not refuse. I will flush the sequestered girlfriend out.

Women eventually have to wee.

Kate finds a bottle of Pinotage, his favourite. Gathering up a corkscrew and two wine glasses, the last of the set of twelve that was Beth's wedding present to them, she goes back to the stoep. She smiles sweetly down at Leonard, her stomach churning. Always the split. Milk and acid.

Look at me, Leonard. She presents herself in front of him. Look how well I am doing. Without you. Because I am without you. I am doing so well I can sit on my stoep and have a glass of wine with you and smile. My body might have been hell bent on betraying me, but my mind has cut right through your bullshit.

Placing the glasses on the table, she gestures to the bottle, inviting him. He looks at the label approvingly and moves to open it.

Where is Daniel? she chafes, wishing he would arrive to insinuate himself upon this scene. She wants Leonard to see that she has other men in her life.

The envelope lies on the table like a white joke.

She takes the bottle from him and pours the wine as an offering or libation to the thwarted and frustrated gods of marriage. Scrabbles in her brain for something to say to delay him.

To our grandsons, toasts Leonard gravely. May they survive this ordeal; no, more than survive, may this be the beginning of two magnificent lives.

Kate decides to drink to that. To life, in all its mysterious guises.

Don't you miss this? He tips his glass at Kate.

Kate glances around, thinking: But I have this, everything that surrounds me.

He gestures to illustrate his meaning, a repetitive loop of the hand, sewing up the space between them.

She wants to remind him of that evening in their kitchen with their child asleep in her room at the end of the passage, when he pleaded: After everything I have given you during all the years of our marriage, please, allow me this one thing. Meaning affairs. Her devotion and contribution rendered invisible.

He still believes a ménage à trois is possible. This time round he is offering his divorced wife the position of mistress.

She wants to laugh, but shakes her head, thinking: No, Leonard, I don't miss what you offer. Her ex-husband cannot see her. It doesn't matter what she says or thinks or does, it doesn't matter if she shakes her head right off, Leonard has his aureole which has already decided the story. He thinks he knows how this will end.

That damn Beethoven cellphone ring again, she fumes. I bet it's the car woman phoning to find out how much longer he'll be. Or the city woman phoning to find out when she can expect him, not knowing about the car woman.

He presses the phone to his ear: Leonard Rycroft.

Kate cannot sit here all day and listen to the great man taking phone calls. She stands, motioning that she has to go, but he gestures for her to wait. Perhaps it's about the twins, so Kate restrains herself, all these differently tuned strings discordant in her. Yes, yes, he says, listening intently, bent slightly over his heart. I know, my darling. It's his Jessica voice. I know. Do you want me to come tonight? I could change my flight.

The envelope lies on the table like an old scar.

Left out, Kate aches. I will go outside and get into Leonard's car and sit with the left-out car woman. I have more in common with her than with this man.

Okay. Okay. Leonard nods. Let me know. Bye, darling, bye now. He switches off, stares up at his ex-wife, looking strained, drained: They're still in theatre.

He could have handed the phone to me, grieves

Kate. He could've told Jess that I am right beside him.

Although, she can't speak to Jess with Leonard's monitoring eye on her. She realises that whatever he does, Leonard can do nothing right because he is wrong for her; he has wronged her. As right as he used to be for her, he has now become someone she needs to avoid for her own mental health. The very same man but also not the same, just as Jess the child is not the same as Jess the adult, and Da the middle-aged farmer has morphed into someone quite unrecognisable.

He adopts his gentle, penetrating voice: Jess and I, we've been talking. I know what the problem is between you. He looks at her. Kate steels herself. Jess is trying to live her own life, he continues. She needs to find out who she is. She can't do that in your shadow. You are too much for her, too powerful. Kate watches as Leonard leans back and positions a cigarette between his lips. He lights up and inhales deeply, preparing: You are like the River Nile putting out Jessica's campfire.

The air is suddenly thick, mucoid. She cannot breathe. Leonard is accusing her of the worst thing any parent can do to their child – extinguish their essence. He is saying that she is guilty of the opposite of nurturing, that instead, she is killing her daughter.

Hold on, Kate, she advises. He himself is afraid of the power of women.

She takes furious aim: I suppose that woman in your car represents an appropriate trickle, Leonard? Or do you go for the stagnant-puddle type nowadays?

He starts, taken aback for a split second, long enough for Kate to catch a flicker of his true expression. He has forgotten about his passenger. Then he recovers, covers up, laughs it all off: Helen! I haven't 'gone' for Helen! She's a student, for god's sake. Kate recalls how his lies made her crazy. I'm giving her a lift.

You should have invited her in then, she says. She has caught him out too many times.

I was just popping in to give you the ticket. The envelope lies on the table between them, a home-made bomb, ticking. Anyway, she is not feeling too well. Migraine.

Layers of lies, spread thickly to smother any green, struggling shoots of truth.

You had better get going then, she says brightly, standing, playing along. Cannot have Helen vomiting in your car. Leonard opens his mouth, but she rushes on: I have goats to milk. And someone is coming over for supper.

He stands, knocking back his wine. Stares at Kate through the cross-hatch of his innocent eyes: You should try sometimes to put your daughter before your goddamn goats.

Get out! Kate is shrieking, but she doesn't care. Let the car woman hear her. Let her know Kate is the bitch that Leonard says she is. Get off my land, get out of my life! And don't ever set foot on my property again with your pathetic little girlfriends!

Kate has picked up the rope. Leonard has dangled it in front of her and she has picked it up and pulled with all her might.

His features have thickened: You are crazy! You can't see what's right in front of you. Always so critical, misreading the situation, then insisting you know what's going on.

For Christ's sake Leonard! Take a long, hard look at yourself before you dare point one cunt-soaked finger at me.

You're disgusting.

Disgusting! Go sell poor Jessica's story to the world. Bask in the spotlight of our misfortune.

You are fucking sick.

I'm not the one who's out there gathering the world's greatest living collection of STDs.

You know absolutely nothing about me anymore. I'm almost a recluse.

Ha! Kate gasps out a crass laugh at this whopper. I've had innumerable reports about your convoluted sex life, not that I am at all interested.

People tell me stuff about you too. I don't necessarily believe it all. I hope most isn't true.

Who? falters Kate. What could he have heard?

He lunges again while she is off balance: You're a control freak, always wanted to control me but you couldn't, so you left. You're doing the same to Jessica.

Control isn't such a bad thing, Leonard. It can keep you from shitting in your pants or unzipping your fly every time there's a woman in front of you.

Leonard is picking up his cellphone, he's heading towards the front door.

Kate is weeping, she can't help herself, great hot tears leaking out of her crumpled, despairing face: You've driven a wedge between me and my daughter.

Leonard swivels round. I am tired of carrying the blame for everything, Ms Holier-than-Thou. How can you think our failed marriage is only my fault. You have never been able to forgive me a couple of affairs, you wear them around your neck like a bloody rosary.

Before Kate can retort that it's a really inappropriate metaphor for an atheist and that she could swear rosaries are not worn around the neck, Leonard steps away into the house, severing the argument. He never abandoned any altercation without the satisfaction of having the last word. The front door bangs hard behind him.

Silence, except for her blood pounding. Kate wipes her face on her sleeve, angry she gave way to tears. Take a look around you, my darling, she reminds herself. This is where you live. This is your new life. He cannot take this away.

Breathe.

The moon is riding higher now, a smudged edge of thumbprint on the wide blue canvas of the sky. To the east is an explosion of cumulus billowing out of dense grey, its plumes seared white by the afternoon sun.

A squirrel weaves its way across the lawn like a

sine wave, then scrabbles up the yellowwood tree. A Cape grassbird calls, and a dove. A sunbird flicks its iridescent plumage in the honeysuckle trellis.

The sound of Leonard's car jars as he roars off.

Leonard came all this way to cut her down. She always kept herself small enough to keep Leonard happy. Now, she can take up as much space as she wants and not feel ashamed. Here, she can be as beautiful and powerful as the Great River Nile; she can go all the way back to a mysterious source, and all the way forward to merge with the communal waters of the sea. She can feel integral to the great cyclic story of life, rather than like an apologetic tributary to an inflated man's flood plain.

Kate picks up the envelope and opens it. Details of an e-ticket. Domestic plane departure is at three forty-five tomorrow to Johannesburg. Then an overnight flight to Heathrow. Acquired, no doubt, on his frequent flier miles.

Leonard knows her well enough to know she won't want to waste this. She slides it back into the envelope and stuffs it into the back pocket of her jeans. Clears up the glasses, takes them through to the kitchen.

The dogs clatter in, expectant. She fills their bowls

with dog chunks and some bread and vegetable remains. Food in, shit out. Feeding the shit machine.

She has spent many years arguing with Leonard inside and outside her head. From now on, she decides, she will not do so. Forgiveness is overrated, she notes, it is a ploy promoted by wrongdoers to keep themselves unrepentant and in circulation. Rather what was done to wrongdoers in the old days – cut off their ears and noses so that everyone can see: Avoid this person. They are not to be trusted.

We might all of us end up noseless and earless, she worries.

Kate has managed to throw Leonard out of her bed and out of her house; she will now throw him out of her thoughts.

Five forty-two and she still hasn't got to the goats. Suddenly Kate feels very tired. The surgeons have been in theatre for over eight hours. Perhaps they take it in shifts, delegating the gentle dissection of fragile tissues to other fresher colleagues.

The dogs scrabble up and bound outside. Arrival of Daniel's bakkie. Brakes, as it comes to a halt. Car doors opening, slamming. The circus has returned. Kate wants to run out to greet her friend and unburden herself of the ordeal that has displaced her peace. Instead she switches on the oven to cook the quiche.

Da blunders in with a bandage around his head.

Daniel is all concern and apologies. Da fell off a stool and hit his crown. He doesn't think stitches are necessary but he offers to take Da through to the hospital if Kate thinks otherwise.

They get Da to sit down for long enough to unwind the bandage. He has a swelling at the back of his head with a messy but superficial wound that has stopped bleeding. The local clinic is only staffed on Mondays and Thursdays and the hospital is over an hour's drive.

Kate wonders whether they are stitching Storm and Sky closed yet, into their own separate skins.

He'll be fine, Kate decides. Da falls all the time.

She could phone now. Right now.

Sharon says: When you get to a fork in the road, take it.

They wrap his head up again. Kate has the urge to wind the bandage down lower, tightly over his mouth to stop the incessant mutter.

Instead she asks: You okay, Da?

He looks at his daughter, perplexed, then stands and wanders out towards the dam, mumbling and plucking at his bandage. Before he reaches the line of trees, he has pulled it off. It falls lightly to the ground, a white flag. Elihle picks up the bandage and folds it carefully. He has been well-schooled in the hazards of blood. He walks on, following her father.

Daniel is looking out of the window after them. Should I –? He makes a start for the door, but Kate touches his shoulder to detain him. His flesh is warm beneath the check of his shirt.

He'll pull it off again. It's not bleeding, so I don't suppose it matters.

Daniel looks different. He has his spectacles on. His eyes get tired at the end of the day, something to do with pollen or heat or dust. He takes his contact lenses out, dons frames, and metamorphoses into a stout professor. He appears vulnerable, hiding behind thick lenses.

He holds out a bottle of red. A good and expensive Shiraz. Kate wants more wine to unwind her, she wants liquid tendrils swirling through her brain.

There's a bottle open already, she offers, gesturing to the Pinotage standing alone on the table on the stoep.

Keep it, Daniel says. He takes up the corkscrew and

screws the metal twist into the cork and extracts it, his large and powerful body intent.

Leonard was here, she explains, not wanting him to think she drinks alone.

Daniel doesn't respond. He never has a point of view about her past life. He likes to live as though they have just been born, untainted by all that went before.

The past and future have dominated her whole day. Only the demented and the Buddhists manage to live fully in the present, she sighs. Da's favourite saying was 'let bygones be bygones'. Now that he has erased his entire past from his brain, his daughter has to deal with it.

It is pointless trying to talk to Daniel about her problems – sweet, emotionally inarticulate man that he is. She gathers up two fresh glasses and leads Daniel out into the afternoon. The light is starting to drain from the sky, which is now the colour of whey.

Daniel tilts the bottle and the wine swills out and settles into the glasses in a red ellipse. He raises his glass, touches it to hers.

Have you heard anything?

Kate shakes her head. It is too soon to celebrate.

Daniel seats himself on the bench next to her. They

sip wine and look out over the dam. Tracks left by the Tripods' vehicle mar the grass. Otherwise the fields still look like those of her childhood.

Her father is standing unsteadily amongst the trees looking up into the canopy, muttering to himself, his hands fidgeting at his sides. His clothes hang off his frame. Elihle squats on the ground near him, scratching with a stick, bored with this life. Kate realises that Elihle will leave her, and Gert is old and will want to retire. She should put Da in an old age home, and train Elihle to do Gert's work. She has to make plans before the future ambushes her.

She knows almost nothing about this young man. He knows almost everything about her. He lives in her house. Kate has never been inside his grandmother's home in the township. He hears what she has to say about everything but never mentions the ideas or plans that must surely roam in his head.

I must ask him what he wants, Kate advises herself.

Da ambles off towards the shed, shouting incoherently. He would have chosen death rather than this ignominious end. An overdose of pills would do it. Quite possible to assume he did it himself in his current state.

Above the house, apricot clouds gather around the smear of the setting sun. Weaver birds are creating a commotion in the reeds as they settle in to roost, checking in with each other after a day of foraging.

The early evening ritual of the birds is soothing. It is a reminder that life continues despite human interference.

Daniel is saying something about his mother coming to stay. His voice is ponderous with duty. His mother is an anxious bore, an emotional recycler. Kate doesn't want to discuss her so she says: Nosisi put a quiche in the oven. Won't you check it please, Dan? I'm going to phone Jessica.

The time has come.

Daniel leaps to his feet to do her bidding. He will do absolutely anything she asks. It is a terrible thing to have such power over someone. They are bound to hate you for it, sooner or later, she thinks.

She takes the handset and leans on the balustrade, looking over the land towards the dam. Something to keep her steady. Before losing impetus, she presses the buttons in the right sequence. Beep, beep, beep. I am not Daniel's mother she reminds herself. Beep, beep, beep. Sharon says if you want to know beep, beep,

beep, whether a man is any good, beep, beep, beep, find out whether he loves his mother. Beep, beep, beep. Beep.

Leonard has a kind and generous mother whom he hardly ever visits.

A pause while the whole system connects, electronic buzzing and whirring through deep sea cables, or flying via satellites through the sky, then: Ring, ring.

What to make of women, ring, ring, who do not love their mothers?

Ring, ring.

Kate holds the phone to her ear, her left hand tucked into her right armpit for comfort. There is movement in the brush near the trees. A mongoose? Da and Elihle are out of sight.

Hello? Jess, speaking across a great divide, although it sounds as though she is right in the room.

Jess.

Mum?

How are they? This has been the longest day. Silence. My darling girl, please, I don't want to find out from your father.

Jess's breath catches, then tears into a sob: Sky didn't make it.

Oh, my darling. Kate wishes she could unravel life to a time before all this. But to what point? Everything was set in motion from way back. Storm?

In intensive care. He's okay, so far.

I have a ticket. Silence. Just say the word, and –

I can't –

Please, there's enough suffering in the world without us adding to it.

It's easier when you aren't around.

Kate takes a deep breath: What must I do? Tell me, please. Your father –

Stop it!

What?

Going on and on about Dad's faults.

Leonard says I'm destroying you, is that really what you think –?

I can't do this right now, for goodness' sake, my baby –

Sorry, I'm so very –

This is not about you, or your divorce –

I know that, please, I tried my best, I always –

There you go again, I can't talk to you. I can't talk to you right now! Jessica cuts her mother off by pressing a button.

Dialling again, Kate has to wait all the way through her rejection message: Hi there, this is Jessica Rycroft. I can't take your call right now but if you'd like to leave a message, please do so after the beep and I'll get back to you as soon as possible.

Jess, please – Kate tries, into the mouthpiece, breathing hard, hard to breathe – I am not the enemy.

The phone listens for a while then goes dead.

Daniel is on the stoep. He comes over, takes the handset from her and places it on the table. His arms reach out and pull her in. Kate tenses. She cannot give him anything except whey and dinner and home-made cheese, but the offered comfort is overwhelming. He has a warm smell, an animal smell of fresh body. Her hunger burrows all the way back to being alone and lonely in boarding school at nine years old. She relaxes into the awkward kindness that is Daniel, sinking into the offering of his body, his farmer's hands applied like large poultices to her back. She is leaking copiously from her face, her eyes, nose, mouth wetting the front of his shirt, the dark mat of his chest hair rough at the vee.

Sorry, Kate sniffs, trying to pull away, but he eases her back into his care.

Sky's gone, she tells him. Storm's in intensive care. That doesn't sound good, does it? Oh, and my daughter hates me.

I'm sorry, he says.

Kate lets this well-meaning, bumbling man hold her. It's been a long time since she has been held with kindness. All she has ever wanted is a happy ending.

Then she feels it: Below the soft bulge of his belly is a hard nub nudging her abdomen. Again she flowers open; a reflex, the response of the body short-circuiting the complicated arguments of the brain.

She longs to be filled.

If life is an experiment, why do I keep choosing restraint? It's life I want, not these dark deaths.

Others do it, she persuades herself. Don't be so picky. Perhaps this is how to solve the problem of sex.

His lips are on her forehead. He is whispering something she can't hear above the thunder in her ears. Something like: It'll work itself out. What is he referring to? she wonders. Sex? Relationships? Surgery?

Daniel is a good man. She lifts her wet face and

offers her mouth like a starving baby bird. His lips are surprisingly firm; they stumble a bit on hers. The tip of his tongue wets her lips, and retreats. A shy invitation.

She slides her tongue into his mouth and he receives her, hesitantly, then the hunger rouses and he has her face between his hands and he is filling her mouth, her hands are on his buttocks, pulling him towards her, wanting to feel his desire more, wanting to feel him want her. His breath is heavy, fast. She wants him to reach into her pants, past the rough hair to the secret place now as wet as her face, but she, too, is shy, caught fighting both her reticence and her desire. He lifts her shirt, finds her breast. She does not resist. She finds the hard rod of his offering; a desperate handhold.

His moan, close to her ear.

There is no afterwards, Kate convinces herself. This is all there is. With this caring man's seed I will wash away my sorrow.

She fumbles with his fly, and he has to help her. They smile sheepishly at each other over this mechanical interruption, and then it is open, and his raw want is in her hand and he has to stop her milking him, his hand holding her wrist hard while his breath grapples with itself.

She wants him to come, she wants his seed all over her. With his semen I will wash Leonard away; this repeats like a mantra.

They are acting as though Da and Elihle are not around. Kate is shocked by her behaviour. Her grandson has just died but she cannot feel it, all she knows is a terrible and overwhelming desire to receive the man who has appeared like an angel before her.

As Kate takes his hand and pulls him into the house, as he hitches his pants up to follow her through the entrance hall and towards her bedroom, she glances into the kitchen where Elihle sits with Da in the circle cast by the overhead light, his elbow on the table, holding a spoon laden with food. Something has changed between them, for Elihle is managing to feed her father.

Their eyes meet; they lock briefly. Kate sees across the entrance hall, through the doorway into the kitchen, across the table, over the spoon and in through the apertures of Elihle's pupils. This young man knows she has a life only because she pays him to forgo his.

Kate turns away and pulls Daniel into her bedroom. What I do in my house is none of Elihle's business, she reasons angrily.

The phone sounds out in the lounge. Hold on, Kate says, in case this is Jessica, come to her senses in the time it has taken for Kate to lose hers.

She fetches the handset from the stoep, keeping her eyes averted from the scene in the kitchen, and goes to the bedroom with it pressed to her ear.

Hello?

Hi. Jessica.

Kate closes the door behind her. Daniel is sitting on her bed in his shirt, his large thighs angling out from under his belly, his bare pink feet flat on the white cotton mat. He has removed his spectacles and cleared a space for them on her bedside table. She doesn't want them there. It looks as though his spectacles have moved in.

Talk to me, my darling.

She goes and stands in front of Daniel, wanting him to anchor her. Daniel looks up at her out of soft eyes, then buries his face into the V of her sex. His hands press her hips to his face. His warm breath heats the insides of her thighs through her jeans.

The problem, Mum, is you think you're always right.

He breathes, breathing her in. The ticket crackles under his hand in her back pocket, so she pulls it out and throws it onto the bedside table.

Do I? Kate cannot argue with her daughter now. She is drugged with want and beyond care.

You are always bossing me, telling me what to do with my life. You are so bloody opinionated.

Well, I am older than you, darling. I happen to know some things –

Daniel places a hand on her belly to soothe her. She strokes his head, his dark curls springing under her hand. He unzips her jeans.

Maybe just listen for a change! You can't possibly know everything!

Kate wants to listen. It's what good mothers do. I'm listening, she manages, as Daniel pulls her jeans down over her bum. She wants him to stop, this is important, but she also wants him to continue. Washing her with his breath. Wanting her for exactly who she is, unlike anyone else in her life.

Then maybe you'd learn something from me!

Jess, I am here for you.

She falls onto the bed next to Daniel and kicks off her gumboots. Daniel is pulling her jeans right off.

You all right, Mum?

I'm fine. I'm so sorry, that's all.

But Kate isn't fine, she is mortified: I have no shame, drunk, but she hasn't drunk enough wine to feel so out of control. She has forgotten, that's all. Forgotten the elixir of sex. Drowning in it, she struggles to the surface and indicates that Daniel should come and lie inside her arm. His hand rests on the inside of her thigh; his fingers touch her through her undies.

Is someone with you?

No. At least, yes. Daniel is with me. Remember Daniel Zimmerman?

Your neighbour?

Yes. Silence. Is that a problem?

Look, I'll speak to you later.

No, wait. Please. Please, tell me about Storm.

A hesitation. He's so little, with these big machines, tubes and wires everywhere.

One of Kate's mother's refrains was: I told you so. She can see it clearly, a hard, red smack on a little hand. I told you so.

Has anyone been with you today, darling?

Chrissie.

Where is the twins' bloody father? If only they had used contraception. Kate had made sure when Jess hit puberty that her daughter knew the basics.

She wants to say: I told you so.

I told you so. I told you so.

Instead, she says: I'm glad you have good friends. Silence. Kate continues so that her daughter won't hang up. Is there anything I can do?

You shouldn't have bought that ticket.

Actually, your father gave it to me.

Silence.

I must go, Jess says and switches off.

Kate is switched off, but Daniel is still a live wire. Oh my god, Kate flagellates herself, I can't believe that Daniel is naked in my bed. This is a big mistake.

He does not read the change in her, but presses his need into her thigh and slips a hand into her undies. His fingers massage her hopefully.

I could go with this, Kate resolves. I could go through with it. I can close my eyes and pretend. I can't say no now. I have to help him.

Poor Daniel.

Poor me.

This is so embarrassing.

He pulls her undies down and her top off, heaving and sweating, then shrugs his shirt off. Kate's old friend Daniel is sitting naked on her bed, his arsehole against her duvet cover, his erection straining against the mound of his belly, his naked glans puce and startling against the hairy white skin of his abdomen.

It is a strange moment when you first see someone naked.

Pippa said that's the first thing she does with her clients – sit cross-legged across from each other, naked. No touching, only looking. Accessing the embarrassment, the shame, the arousal, the pain.

Daniel levers himself on top of her and nudges his way in.

Oh, Kate, Kate!

It is over in two minutes, but Kate is grateful. She is certain Elihle heard Daniel attain Nirvana.

Daniel buries his face in her hair until his breathing evens. She is panting too, but only because she can hardly breathe beneath the bulk of him.

Somehow she has to get him out of there.

He rolls off her, pulls her to him.

Did you –? He looks at her pleadingly, asking for help. Are you –?

Gently Kate extracts herself. I really need to wee, she explains.

She goes to the bathroom and closes the door,

not wanting him to hear her tinkle. It's my fault, she castigates. My one good friend in the area. We'll never be able to look at each other again.

Poor Daniel.

Poor me.

It's obvious, she decides. The pink bathmat has to go. She has always hated it. Tomorrow she will give it away to Nosisi. She can no longer live with the folly of pink.

Daniel's teaspoonful of spent pleasure slides out of her and drops into the bowl.

Kate wipes him away, stands and pulls a brush through her hair. She notes in the mirror that her skin no longer fits around her eyes and there are sun blemishes on her right temple. Her breasts hang slightly, but they are good breasts. There is that niggle that perhaps they carry the seed of the curse that grew in her mother's. Kate has not been for a mammogram for many years.

Her daughter waits with engorged breasts over her surviving child.

A weight tethers Kate to the impasse.

Oh, god, she sighs, there is a man in my bedroom. A moment of weakness. As though we can control sex and feeling. As though we are in control.

What to do.

She grabs a towel and wraps it around her. Deep breath. Enter the bedroom.

Daniel has inserted himself under her covers. Her duvet is covering his nethers but his chest full of hair protrudes. He holds out his arms, but she doesn't know whether she even likes him anymore. The tragic unravelling of so much in a few unguarded moments.

She sits on the edge of the bed.

Leonard bought me a ticket. She gestures to the envelope. To travel with him to London tomorrow.

The phone rings. It's probably Leonard phoning to tell her that Sky is dead. Animated flesh rendered suddenly inert.

Must I? Daniel's hand hovers over the phone.

Leave it. Come and eat. She pulls on her jeans under the towel, careful not to reveal more of herself than necessary. Putting on a jacket against the evening chill, she leaves Daniel to his process of dressing and goes through to the kitchen.

Ah, Mary! her father says, looking up. You're looking wonderful this morning.

He never complimented her mother while she was still alive.

Kate should document this bizarre time, write it all down so that she remembers after everything has changed once again as it always eventually does.

But Leonard is the writer. He knows how to seduce with words, how to manipulate the reader in such a manner that she does not suspect that something is being done to her, falling into the arms of his books, believing in the fabrications he so expertly creates.

Come, Da. Sweet how Elihle has started calling her father Da. He wipes her father's mouth and helps him up from the table. Elihle, with his innocent skin. None of the cruel things that have happened to him have been his fault.

He leads Da through to the hallway and up the stairs, Da protesting that he has not yet milked the cows. The cows have gone, Da, she sighs, making way for golf, remember? One monoculture giving way to another that's still further removed from what naturally exists. Nature as scenery, as repository for the skilful positioning of small white balls. Wild creatures, insects and plants have been destroyed to make way for pastures and fairways. We never noticed these other signs of life before, now we don't miss them at all. 'The curse of usefulness', Brecht wrote, referring to trees.

If anything in nature does not have a monetary value, we let it go extinct. Milking the land for pleasure and profit. Milking the land dry.

The quiche is perfect, firm and hot and fragrant with a crisp crust, but Kate's stomach shows no interest. Daniel comes into the room, bringing the wine in from the stoep, sheepishly. They sit at the table, awkward and apologetic with each other.

He pours the wine while Kate cuts him a large slice. Thank you, he says, with emphasis. She is not sure what he's referring to.

How to get through this meal. Kate feels violated, but it is she who has violated herself. She should have said no, spoken out, not given herself up so easily. In the shadow below the wooden rectangle of the table top, her sex is still a confusion but above the table she is quite clear. Daniel thinks her withdrawal from him is because of his poor performance as a lover.

She puts her fork down, leaving her slice of quiche

half-eaten. Sometimes the body knows when to stop, she thinks.

Daniel helps himself to salad. Clearing his throat, he announces: If you are pregnant, I'll stand by you and the baby.

Kate is horrified. Daniel forces a smile, and she realises that, of course, she is past having babies, hasn't menstruated for a year, and that this is a joke. She went straight back to that place fertile women know well – the fear of falling pregnant.

He blunders on: I would've loved to have had a baby with you, you know. I think you are the most wonderful mother.

He mouths the words Kate wanted to hear her whole married life. She catches herself, before feeling too grateful. Having a baby is a way men can make women dependent.

Kate resumes eating her quiche fast without tasting, wanting dinner to end so Daniel can go home. I'm sorry, she says, about what happened. I didn't mean –

He waves her explanation away. I know, he says, his voice breaking. Pushing his plate away, Daniel puts his elbows on the table and buries his face in large farmer hands. He pulls a white, crumpled hanky out of his pocket and presses it to his eyes, but it doesn't help. Great heaving sobs.

He is about to find out that I am not a wonderful mother, Kate riles. That's enough! she wants to say. For god's sake, pull yourself together. You're like a little boy who has had his sweeties taken away.

It isn't personal, Daniel. She tries for a gentle tone. I'm just not, it's not –

He nods, wipes his eyes roughly and resumes eating, too much, too fast, keeping his gaze averted. His face, looking down, is almost angelic with his dark eyelashes.

It's my fault, he says between mouthfuls, still looking at his plate. I was stupid to think that someone as beautiful as you could want someone like me.

Well that, Daniel, Kate wants to say, is exactly the problem. I need a man with good self-esteem, so I don't have to prop him up.

Instead she says: You're really great, Daniel. But you're like a brother to me. Which is better, in many ways, don't you think?

Daniel lowers his fork onto the plate. I brought ice cream. It's in the fridge, he offers as recompense, needing sweetness to soothe him. There is something dark wedged between his front teeth.

Thanks Daniel, but I can't eat much right now.

It's home-made, he protests.

My stomach is in a knot. It's been a hell of a day.

He accepts this as he accepts everything. Daniel is a workhorse, a great gelding of a cart horse, powerful, reliable. Boring. She wants a stallion. But stallions, she knows, are too akin to Prince Charming, and men who are charming cannot be trusted. She's caught in her own web.

Daniel, can you do something for me?

Of course. His whole body lights up.

I still haven't got to the goats.

Sure. He stands, ready to rush out into the darkness to help with the milking.

I'll see to the goats. It's about letting people know. Kate reaches for the address book under the phone. Please, Dan, call Pippa and Beth. And Margaret. Tell them that Sky didn't make it. That Storm is in ICU. And Sharon, please phone Sharon, tell her I'll ring her first thing tomorrow. I can't phone anyone right now.

Daniel nods. Forlorn. I can take you to the airport tomorrow, he offers.

Everyone but Jess wants her to go.

Thanks. Just do that phoning, okay?

She hesitates, then proceeds with the expected. Gives Daniel a hug, quick enough so she doesn't feel a thing. I'll let you know about tomorrow, she says and shoves a box of matches into her pocket, takes up the milk pails and paraffin lamp and goes out of the back door.

It is a relief to be outside under the expanse of night, reduced to an ant traversing the thin layer between earth and sky. Focussing on this small, important task. Down the path to the goats.

The surgery has released Storm into a normal life, yet solving problems is never easy. She is aware of survivor guilt, that the death of his twin will shape Storm's life in some unpredictable way.

The twilight raucous of birds has given way to night sounds, frogs and crickets taking their turn on the air waves, calling out for mates across the void.

Daniel's spermatozoa are still wriggling, desperate and perplexed, inside her. Frustrated vectors of desire on every level. If I were still fertile, Kate admonishes herself, I could have fallen pregnant on the day one of Jess's children died. She would never have forgiven me, correctly so.

It occurs to her that there may be other wrigglys inside her. As far as Kate knows, Daniel has been celibate for years. Perhaps he is one of those men who has a secret sex life – connecting with dodgy types through the internet, or when he goes to town for stock or deliveries.

The ovum of the moon falls slowly through the ejaculate of the Milky Way towards the western horizon. Millions of people all over the world are making love right now, or having sex or fucking – insert whatever word – penetrating perhaps, trying to infiltrate, permeate and comprehend the mystery of another person or themselves, trying to find release, to be understood, to conquer, punish, comfort, or to make babies; not understanding what they are doing and what will come their way as a result of conjoining in this impetuous, compulsive, calamitous climax. Thus are lives made and subsumed, marauded, voided; thus, we lurch forward on our haphazard consummate way.

The goats have either heard or smelt Kate coming. They bump against the gate, bleating and stamping their hooves, complaining to the management about the lateness of the hour. Their udders are swollen, and their bellies empty, anticipating their ration of pellets. She opens the gate, careful not to let Oupa slip in. The wayward old goat needs to go for the ultimate chop. She calls the others into the milking enclosure and they come, pushing and butting past each other in their haste. Counts until all thirty-four have entered. Shuts the gate to contain them.

One foot in front of the other, so tired, pushing through the bleating mass of goats to the goat hok. Enters and shuts the door, enclosing herself, alone in utter darkness. Fumbles for the wide shelf at the back, places first the paraffin lamp on its surface, then the milk pails. The rub of her jacket as she makes these movements. Grapples with a box of matches. Lights the lamp. The warm flame takes, flinging her shadow up the wall. Finds the jar and short length of hosepipe that Gert keeps stashed in the corner.

Fills the fodder bucket with pellets. Life goes on, she warns herself; we must go on. At the sound of the hard pellets pelting against the metal, the goats increase their chorus. Kate stands the bucket at one end of the milking table. Her body performs the routine as though a mechanism were operating her joints. Opens the small door at the top of the ramp to let the first goat in and onto the table.

Hennie. Always Hennie, butting her way to the front. First up the steps and in through the door. She nudges Kate in greeting, sticks her head into the bucket. Whitie is trying to push her way in too, so Kate puts a hand against her chest, shoves her backwards and bolts the small door. One at a time. Hennie is eating as fast as she can while Kate squirts the first dry milk plug laced with bacteria and dirt from the two tense teats into the jar, then brings the milk pail in under her. She grips each teat between her fingers and thumbs and begins coaxing the liquid out of the animal in long full squirts, the white fluid drilling and frothing against the side of the metal pail.

Sky would have died anyway, she soothes her ache, whether I'd been there or not.

A slight odour rises from the bucket, sweet and warm, unlike the pungent goat smell which develops a few days after the milking. She likes Hennie, a beautiful animal with spirit, sometimes too much spirit; Kate must watch her so that she does not overturn her efforts.

Beth has commented that it is not accidental that they are associated with the devil. Cloven hoof, horns, bony heads with strange yellow eyes, the pupil slits going vertically across. The angular shoulders and hip bones jutting like pegs to suspend the pendulous belly. Scapegoats, pack animals for our projections. Carrying the sins of humans – having their throats cut or being sent into the wilderness to die.

There will be a funeral. Kate realises she will have to go over for the funeral.

She butts the warm bag of the udder with the backs of her hands, mimicking a young suckling kid who instinctively knows how to evoke another let-down of milk. Slowly the streams become shorter and the udder slackens. Kate opens the second small door that leads from the milking table back to the field and hits the goat's buttocks lightly with the hose.

Uit! she commands. These goats have been brought up by Gert, and only understand Afrikaans. Hennie is reluctant to relinquish the food so Kate has to strike her again, a quick sting to the buttocks. Greedy gits, she observes. These animals feed all day on the lushest pastures in the world, yet they regard the pellets as the real treat. Like children, who prefer a factory-made chocolate bar to a freshly picked apple. Makes you wonder, she wonders, what they put in processed foods to make us crave them, although these expensive pellets contain no unnatural additives so that her cheese can qualify as organic.

Hennie scrambles down the ramp back into the field. Kate closes the door and opens the other. Kom! she commands. Whitie puts her head through and pulls herself into the hok, her front hooves scrabbling in her haste to get to the bucket.

Squirt the first milk into the jar. Slip the pail in. Long slow tugs on the teats, keeping the movements rhythmic.

Sometimes Kate is bored by this slow routine as the animals pass through her hands one after another. Tonight, this round is comforting. It harnesses her body to a repetitive act as familiar as breathing; it provides limits for her grief, penning it in. She is grateful for the focus her animals provide on this day.

If she had lived in times past, she would have offered a goat as sacrifice to ensure a good outcome for the twins. If she had believed in these practices, Fate might have been kinder and Sky might still be alive. If she had prayed to Jesus, would that have helped?

Son of God was also the Lamb of God. But she is sure people used goats more often than lambs for sacrifice in those impoverished desert lands. Jesus as Goat of God. Jesus as lamb sacrifice, Satan as goat. Good and evil, conjoined. One cannot exist without the other, like birth and death.

Uit! Whitie skedaddles.

Kom! In comes Bonny, all scrawny legs, angular head and udder. These goats and her dogs are usually the only living things she touches.

A crack sounds loudly outside, a dry branch breaking. In the direction of the trees. Kate stops, listens. The night air is singing with frogs and insects. A moth flicks itself against the glass of the lamp.

Bonny munches on.

Kate waits, straining her ears.

Daniel? she calls. No reply. She has not yet heard his bakkie leave.

Those words uttered by the sketchbook-snatcher: Aren't you afraid, living alone here? That was the subject of Leonard's last book. A woman living alone, vulnerable, on a South African farm.

She continues milking, her breath shallow as she listens, alert, aware of how alone she is in a small hok in the dark, far from the house. She could run for it, Daniel is still inside her home.

The dogs have not barked a warning. She must be imagining things.

At the very least she should have a bolt on the door. Perhaps give in to Sharon's nagging to buy a cellphone for security.

Kom! The goats move on: one out, another one in.

Kate has decided never to read one of her ex-husband's books again. In *The Fallen,* an astronomer, reluctantly leaving the observatory in Sutherland and returning home to the city and a turbulent marriage, decides to take a break from his trip. He books into a guest cottage on a farm owned by a lonely farmer, Carmen, who invites him for a supper of Karoo lamb bredie. Over a bottle of wine, he tells her about the stars, seducing her with his passion for what he has seen in the heavens. A car drives up, the dogs bark. There are gunshots, and silence. Four intruders tie the astronomer to a chair. He is forced to watch while the men rape the woman, this stranger he himself has all evening been subtly trying to persuade into bed. His mode is seduction and manipulation in order to extract permission. Now he is made to watch while the intruders take what they want.

Uit!

Kom!

Afterwards, with the phone lines cut and the intruders having driven off with their valuables in their cars, the two have to decide whether to blunder out into the terror of the night, or to stay locked in and wait for morning. Leonard has imagined a false response from the fictional woman. She asks the man to make love to her. It is clear, Kate fumes, that her ex has never been raped. He does not begin to understand the horror and the shame and the rage and the blame attendant on such a violation.

Uit! Kom!

Old thoughts loop and snag. She is incensed by male writers fabricating a woman's response in these false ways. When Kate confronted Leonard, he explained patiently that he was exploring a man's impotence in a country as complex as South Africa. A man who cannot protect a woman carries huge guilt, he said. It castrates him. That was why his protagonist could not make love to her.

Kate could not get Leonard to see that hatred, disgust and fear of women is endemic to our culture, nor how that trope is apparent in the machinations of his imagination.

Uit!

Kom!

She stops to listen past the sounds of the night for any further movement, not able to shake off the feeling that something or someone is outside. Death, she reminds herself, remembering to breathe, is always waiting just out of sight of our busy lives.

When she was date-raped at seventeen, Kate was such an innocent. The most common kind of rape, they say, is by a man known to you. In her case, a friend's friend kept filling up her glass at a party until she was drunk, and then he drove her back to his flat and took what he wanted. Help yourself to the woman who has just passed out, no permission needed. The hearth home of her body invaded, ransacked.

Kom!

The sound of an owl. Her heart lifts, and she wants to go outside to stand in her presence. Perhaps she would be rewarded by seeing her mate as well. But she is not even halfway through milking. Tired, so tired. Strong tugs. Butt the udder. Tug, tug. Tug, tug. Butt. Tug, tug. The geneticist has become a milk maid, a term from the days when it was impossible for a woman to become a farmer. Kate recognised early on that power resided in boys but was puzzled as to what exactly the little worm between their legs had to do with this. It was an intriguing appendage but hardly one that suggested power, unless power was measured by how far you could pee.

Kom!

Adrianne, one of the best. Her udder is so full she can barely walk. These animals are in her service but she serves them well, too. It's a trade-off, she's explained to them, domestic animals earn their food, shelter and protection from predators in exchange for giving her their milk.

Don't kick, Adrianne! scolds Kate. At least you are not genetically modified, hey! At least you are a natural old she-goat. The animal isn't listening. Concentrate, Adrianne. This is important. You need to know what our clever species has come up with. Goats that produce milk containing spider web protein so that we can harvest it easily. Scientists have extracted the gene that switches on silk production in spiders, and have inserted it into an ovum of a goat.

You might want to ask why anyone would want to mess with your genes, Adrianne. Because naturally occurring spider silk is the strongest, lightest fibre there is. Its tensile strength is such that a three-centimetre-wide strand could stop an aeroplane in mid-flight. Impressive. But they can't farm spiders, like they do silkworms, because spiders are too antisocial to be farmed in the way silkworms are. Spiders are less compliant than goats.

Klaar. You are empty, empty of all your pure, ungenetically-modified, non-silk milk. Off you go!

Kom! Goeienaand, Julie! As I was saying, important goats, ones unlike yourself, real, science-based, GM goats, can produce the building blocks for this natural fibre, which some corporate person has named Biosteel. Biosteel has quite a ring to it, don't you think? It will be used in applications where lightness and strength are essential – squirt, squirt; squirt, squirt – for example, aircraft and racing vehicles. And bullet-proof clothing.

Compliant, complacent, Afrikaans-speaking Julie-goat is more interested in pellets than the future of her kind. Uit!

Kom!

Klippie, always a bit sheepish, Kate notes, all these animals that she has come to know so well, all with their own distinctive character.

Kate's voice is her protection, keeping the night at bay, the impenetrable night that laps at the edges of the lamplight: Another advantage of spider silk protein, Klippie, unlike many other kinds of protein, is that it's compatible with the human body. She adopts her teacher voice so they cannot complain that she did not warn them. That is good news for humans. No allergic reactions. Tell me truly whether this is bad or good news for you. Aren't you glad to be of service? Biosteel has many medical applications. It will be used for strong, tough artificial tendons, for ligaments and limbs, also for tissue repair and to create super-thin sutures for ophthalmology and neurosurgery.

Kom!

Springertjie. By her slack udder, Kate knows that Gert has been back sometime this afternoon to milk her antibiotic-laced produce. Her teat is still inflamed but it's too soon for the medicine to have taken effect.

Uit, you've had your turn.

Duiweltjie. Another bucket-kicker, irascible. The goat knows that if she creates a disturbance, she can engineer a longer turn at the pellets. She stands tense, taut, tail flicking, her head in the bucket, gobbling.

There! She kicks, nearly upsetting the milk pail.

It's pointless objecting, Kate tells her. We have been using genetically modified *E.Coli* for decades to produce insulin. It's the new slavery. Neither goats, nor any living creature or plant can escape this fate. The great complexity of intricate Mother Nature is harnessed and chained by her DNA to the advancement and health of human beings. Not all humans, mind you. Only those who have already taken more than most. This new technology is mainly for the wealthy chosen few.

Milked dry. Uit!

Kom! Kom!

Gerry, a shy she-goat. One that Kate has to coax into the hok, showing her the contents of the bucket before she clatters up the last step and comes inside. Eat up, Gerry, there's a girl. Talking to one goat is much the same as talking to another. Kate imagines that they spread the news, so by the time she is done with milking, the entire herd has the whole picture – the history of genetics to date. Loss and greed and violation and death so that, for the most part, a select few can continue their bad habits into an old age measured in coffee spoons.

Damage. Damage to the mother, the core of life from which we all emerge, to which we're all connected.

You've heard about the insertion of a salmon gene into the DNA of strawberries? It renders strawberries less susceptible to frostbite. Amazing, isn't it? Imagine, the casual transfer of an animal gene into a plant nucleus. Most scientists are excited and awestruck by these developments, whereas I, I am horrorstruck.

Uit!

Kom!

The mantra of milking.

Some regard me as an old-fashioned, superstitious spoiler. I should be exhilarated by the brilliance of these feats which enable the feeding and healing of human beings. One of these technical advancements might have contributed to saving Storm's life today.

Something in me quails at the way we are tampering irreversibly with the mysterious matrix of nature in our quest for – what exactly? Perfection, immortality?

Nobel prizes?

Genoeg. Kom!

Suzie. Poor producer. Empty udder. Out you go.

Kom!

You'll remember Dolly, Kate reminds Minna, as she presses the first milk of each teat into the jar. Dolly was the first cloned mammal – a sheep. Not far off your kind. Dolly was made from a mature nucleus from a sheep's bladder cell inserted into an enucleated ovum from a different sheep. The switched-off genes switched themselves back on again, and – voilà! – a fertilised ovum.

Uit, my darling.

Kom! Potjie skitters in, her eyes furtive, her jaw working. It's all right, skattebol. Kom hier. Grief is wiping itself through Kate again so she keeps going. She needs her outrage to keep focussed: Prior to this, Potjie, a fertilized ovum could only be created through mating, from the fusing of gametes released by two adults.

Uit. Kom!

Ruth. Stumbling in. Dear old goat.

Squirt, squirt. Ruthie, tell me, wragtig, if it is true that for every gain there is a loss, what have we lost here? Is it okay for a geneticist to engineer a hairless, glow-in-the-dark rabbit for the amusement of his children? It has happened, you know. Now that we can create DNA, is it acceptable to manufacture brand new viruses? We have inadequately and inexpertly failed to weigh up the consequences of these actions, both the harm and the benefit. We have failed to assess the ramifications in every sphere – material, psychological, spiritual. Geoff would argue that DNA is protein, that we are merely moving protein around.

What do you think, Ruth? Are you a lump of protein, an object of exploitation, experimentation and manipulation?

That's it, skattie. You're done.

Kom! Kom Sakkie, jou beurt.

Of course, I am a hypocrite. If my child were dying, I would slaughter the last animal on earth, even you, Sakkie. I would manipulate the final gene in order to save her.

Oh, Jess! One son gone, the other at the brink, your breasts brimful with milk. You'll be expressing for your living son, pumping out the life-giving fluid, full of the nourishment and antibodies he needs to heal. Milk of human kindness.

No use feeling sorry, not for the twins, separated at the fork of life and death, not for Jess, not for Daniel, nor herself. Keep busy, keep idle thoughts at bay.

Kom! Bella, with her skew horn like her mother before her. Bella, listen up. These are the facts. Humans treat nature like a shopping mall, or factory. Or we see nature as a projection of the human condition: nature as wise or vulnerable, savage or bountiful.

Maak klaar, jou vraat.

Kom, Nel! Staan stil.

Or we treat nature as a zoo. Oooh, look at that beautiful butterfly, or elephant, or orchid, we'd better look after it by fencing it off and glassing it in, protecting and managing it so that our grandchildren can pay at the turnstile to see what a real giraffe looks like. We forget: We are part of this thing we have tamed and cordoned off. We fail to care for the natural world that exists outside the reserves.

Uit!

Kom! Sneeukop, a good producer. Luister, I am on a pluck. Squirt, squirt. Is everything on earth natural, including the human capacity to devise and create completely new elements on the periodic table? We are, after all, products of evolution. If that has naturally led to humans creating new life forms, then perhaps there is nothing to be concerned about. Or have we managed to divorce ourselves from nature through the use of our clever brains?

Uit, Sneeukop!

The first pail is full enough. Take it out, place it on the shelf, position the lid.

Kom! Plaatjie. Extract the first milk into the jar, slide the empty second pail under her.

Plaatjie, tell me should we treat you better? You animals don't have a hope of changing your circumstances, because you don't have the means to protect yourselves from humans. Even if you had guns or bombs – the usual methods humans employ to settle differences – you don't have hands. You can't even communicate with us around the negotiating table to put your case forward.

I suspect we have failed you. Our imaginations have failed you.

Kom! Queenie, her biggest she-goat, squeezing through the door, with an udder fit to burst.

That's it, my girl. Eat up. Squirt, squirt, squirt. The distant sound of Daniel's bakkie starting up and heading for home.

Regret, remorse, such unhelpful emotions. Guilt too, a great, black, sucking hole.

Kom! Tiny enters. Hoe gaan dit? Kate asks her. Tiny, who is tiny in all regards except for her udder which yields the richest milk. Kate rests her forehead against her warm flank as she milks, almost swooning with grief and exhaustion.

Squirt, squirt. Wrung out. Unfit to make decisions. Where to go, what to do.

What will become of me, when I am Da's age? Jess might have sold this farm to the Tripods by then and turned me over to a home for senile delinquents.

At least I have done the right thing by Da, she reasons, no matter what Beth says, stupid bitch. If there is one good thing I have done in my life, it is this. I am a good-enough daughter.

Kom!

Uit! Oupa, trying his luck at the pellet pail. How did he get in? Sorry, ou boet, you don't have the necessary equipment for this kind of exploitation. Kate whips him out of the exit gate.

Kom!

Fanny enters. Hoe gaan dit, ou maatjie? The goat that almost died at birth.

Sky is dead. Life moves on. Another child, another goat, gone. It happens, has happened before, many times. That graveyard she visited while in Prince Albert for one of Leonard's book readings, filled with rows of small graves. A plague, no doubt. A Pied Piper, who took all the babies.

Sky was the smaller, the more placid one. Peacefulness or diminutive size might count against one in the race for survival.

A knock.

Kate stops milking. Someone is at the door.

Who would knock, out here in the night? Nobody. Must be a branch in the wind. But there is no wind. Her heart is thumping; she is already checking ways to escape. The small door for the goats that leads to the field – it's too narrow for her to get through in a hurry. Not if someone bursts into the goat hok with intent. No way to lock herself in. Where are the dogs? There was no warning bark.

Kate hesitates, waiting. There it is again, without

a doubt, a knuckle rapping against the wood, not a metre away. Don't be ridiculous, Kate, rapists and murderers don't knock. That woman at lunch put things in your head. That, combined with Leonard's nasty revenge fantasy of what happens to women who leave their husbands and live on a farm alone.

Bugger that. Kate twists the knob and pulls the door open. Light from the lamp spills out and catches starkly on the white smears on the semblance of a face, a mask: too white, unnaturally so, with dark hollows for the eyes, nostrils and mouth. Kate's breath catches as she quickly, reflexively, moves to close the door, close the door! He is pushing in, ducking his height through the frame, his body pushing against her efforts to repel him, and he is inside the hok, and the door bangs closed behind him. It is a him, close, so close to her, she smells his wood smell, his dark eyes glinting a foot away from hers.

It's okay, he breathes. Ssssh, Miss Kate, it's only me.

Kate's hand is pressed to her mouth, Oh, oh Luzoko! Jeez, you gave me a fright.

Ssssh, please, Miss Kate, please, don't make a noise. Sorry, I was waiting outside, I thought there was someone in here, with you. I heard voices.

In her mind's eye Kate can see it, this makeshift goat hok shelter that drifts, lost, like a vessel in the midst of the unstable rural night, emitting only a smidgeon of light and the rambling, raving voice of a woman disturbed by the world. Laughter shakes and gasps out of her.

Oh, Luzuko! She explains: It's what happens when you live by yourself. You start talking to goats. Relief flushes through her. I'm so glad it's you, you're all right? What are you doing here?

If the Frenchmen saw him below the bridge before lunch, he has walked a long way, maybe eight kilometres, she calculates and says: I thought you weren't allowed –

Great sobs of mirth are gathering again under Kate's diaphragm, but Luzoko is not laughing. Something is wrong.

He shakes his head. Please, you are busy. Finish. He steps into the corner near the door. Sits down, very carefully, like an old man, grasping handholds, lowering himself slowly.

Have you hurt yourself?

He waves a hand to indicate that Kate should continue her task. Fanny still has her head in the bucket, more interested in guzzling as much as she can than in attackers in the night.

Genoeg! Weg is jy! A sting with the hose to get her moving again.

Kom! Only two more to go. She continues, puzzled by her visitor. Kom! Kom! Arabella next, nosing her way into the hok. The one with the damaged ear from the caracal attack that left four goats dead. Arabella survived, but nearly died giving birth. Kate was there, she was the one who pulled the newborn out, reaching right inside the mother for a leg. You owe me, Kate has told her, and she obliges, milk by the litre.

The sound of Luzoko breathing behind her, short and shallow. Kate wants to question him but concentrates on coaxing the milk. Staan stil! Squirt, squirt. Butt. Squirt, squirt. The milk drills and foams in the bucket.

She glances over at the young man. He is leaning back against the sacks of pellets propped against the hok wall, his eyes closed, his knees angling out, hands resting on his knees, his chest rising and falling in quick breaths. There's a sheen of sweat on his face.

Uit! Almost finished. For today. Tomorrow it all starts up again.

Kom, Sterretjie! Morning and evening, she's always last on this milking treadmill.

Focus, get this job done. What next, Kate thinks, so tired. Tug, tug. Luzoko must have an infection. The hospital is an hour's drive away. A double espresso to smack her brain awake and they'll be on their way. Kate is the resource here; she is the local taxi service for those who would otherwise die. The ambulance can take two days, often arriving only in time to remove the dead.

Resentment clots in her. A self-inflicted injury gone septic, or pneumonia from sleeping out in the rain, all for some idea about what it is to be a man, and she becomes implicated. She is crazy to be living out here, trying to bridge the lands of superstition and science.

This is not Luzoko's fault.

Uit!

She bolts the door to the field after Sterretjie is out, puts the lid on the pail, and turns to Luzoko, who hasn't moved, propped up in the corner with his head tilted back, eyes closed, his mouth slightly open.

Luzoko? He opens his eyes as Kate presses the back of her hand to his forehead. It is burning hot through the thick smear of white clay. He licks at his cracked lips. This is the son of Nosisi, this boy who grew up playing in the sloot from the weir, who as a small child helped her plant vegetables. Who thought he was helping when he carefully filled up the holes Kate had dug to plant potatoes. This young man who now comes to her for help.

Wait, I'll fetch the bakkie.

That rouses him. No, he protests urgently, standing shakily, steadying himself: I need an injection. His breath is hot and sour.

An injection. Kate understands. Luzoko has seen her treat an infected goat. I can't do that. You need to see a doctor. You probably need to be in hospital on a drip.

He shakes his head, adamant. A trickle of sweat slicks down his temple. He is shivering.

At the hospital, the nurses will talk, other patients will see me. Everyone will know.

Know what? That you are very ill, and that you are being sensible and getting treatment! Kate doesn't have time for this argument.

Luzoko sinks down again. It is a miracle he made it on foot this far.

They will know I did not do it alone.

Kate crouches, trying to get him to look into her face. Luzoko, listen to me. I am not a doctor. I am not even a vet. I don't know how to treat anything other than my own goats. One injection would not be enough for a man.

Then give me two. Two injections, then I'll be okay. His eyes shine, bright with fever. I won't go to the hospital. You must treat me here. Now, tonight.

This sounds like delirium, although he is very serious. He is so ill she could probably force him into the bakkie. He is a tall young man and a fit soccer player. Even if she managed to wrestle him into the cab, Kate is unsure whether you are allowed to abduct and treat someone against their will.

He is staring at her, sweat again beading his brow. You must not tell my mother, he instructs.

It might be TB, Kate argues. The antibiotics I have won't work. Or tick bite fever. It could be tick bite fever. Or –

It's the cut, he says.

Kate hesitates. Look, come to the house and I'll –

No! Said with such vehemence. Please, bring the injections here.

It's Elihle, Kate realises. His friend may not see him.

Dear, kind Elihle, who she cannot imagine would think badly of his friend for seeking help.

Luzoko regards Kate pleadingly, and she is taken back ten years when as a child he could manipulate sweets out of her with those big eyes. I came to you because I may not go to my mother, he says. Of course, Nosisi could easily take syringes out of Kate's drawer. Kate knows that mothers would do anything to save their children. For love of my mother, please do this for me.

Your mother would want me to take you to the hospital, you know that. Come, you are not thinking straight. Kate opens the door. Outside, the moonlight is a soft film lying over the fields. She blows out the paraffin lamp, picks up the milk pails, and indicates that he should follow her. He stands, to her relief. He is, after all, going to be sensible.

Through the muddy, churned up enclosure, through the gate, Luzoko follows, closing it behind him. She starts down the path to the house, walking in the milky moonlight, a pail in each hand. Heavy, so heavy. It was a good yield tonight. I need a cup of coffee and we'll be off, Kate says. No response, so she turns. Luzoko has peeled away and is walking off, stiffly and slowly, up the drive. Leaving.

Hey! Kate calls, setting the pails down. He does not stop, so she runs after him. Just where do you think you're going? He ignores this, keeps walking, keeping his eyes down, breathing hard. I'm talking to you!

Please, Miss Kate, please be quiet.

Luzoko, I will scream my head off if you don't stop this instant!

He stops. Looks at her out of that white mask.

How can you put me in this position? It's not fair.

Luzoko shrugs. Life is not fair, he says without emphasis, looking over her shoulder, past all that is inconsequential, towards the berg. I came here to ask you for the injection. You have said no. That is all.

Luzoko turns to walk away. She understands that he would rather die than face humiliation.

Okay. Alright. You win. Go back to the hok. I will fetch the medicine.

She turns angrily, walks to the pails, picks them up and continues to the house. What did Nosisi say? God has the overview. Only when she is almost at the back stoep does she allow herself to check. Yes, he has walked back and is letting himself in at the gate of the goat hok.

The dogs run happily out to greet her as though she has returned from a journey. Where were you? Kate chides. But they know Luzoko too well. Down, Brutus! If you dare make me spill one drop. Into the kitchen. Pails on the table, ladle some milk into the sterile bottle; she must do this now or it will be forgotten. Add the culture into the bottle of milk, put the bottle into the oven at thirty degrees to incubate overnight. Milk pails into the cold room.

Kate washes her hands thoroughly. Like a surgeon, preparing. She goes through to the study and takes two pre-filled syringes out of the drawer. Life is not fair, she deliberates, but he is probably right. Two doses of long-acting penicillin might do the job, and restore some version of justice.

He could have an allergic reaction, worries Kate. Then she'll have to try to explain a dead young man in the goat hok to the police. Or if he doesn't respond to the antibiotic and dies, she'll go to jail for diagnosing and treating beyond her capabilities.

Through to the bathroom to look in the cabinet. Gauze swabs. Disinfectant. A plastic cup is the right shape. Antiseptic cream. Vaseline. Bandage. Scissors. Pain-killers – anti-inflammatories. Her headlight, kept for power outages. Never dreamt she would get to use it for its original purpose – surgical procedures.

Through to the kitchen to get a basket to contain these supplies, feeling like Florence Nightingale going out onto the battlefield without proper equipment.

Water. He looks dehydrated. Take a bottle from the fridge. Bananas, ham, the bread left over from lunch, and cheese. Mother food for an ill child. Precisely what he is supposed to be escaping. Choose shame, or choose death.

Fill the mug with hot water. Then out through the back door, making her way along the path to the goat hok, carrying the laden basket and the plastic mug. It will have to do. No more deaths today, she prays.

In the goat hok, Kate lights the paraffin lamp. Luzoko is lying on his side on the straw with his arm under his head as a pillow. She puts the basket and mug down and takes out the bottle of cold water.

Drink. He sits up as Kate hands him the anti-inflammatory tablets and the water. It will help the pain and fever.

He looks at the two red pills she has put into his palm. Not necessary, he says. Only the injections.

Kate loses patience. Take them, dammit! I have the

antibiotic right here. If you want to get better, listen to me.

Luzoko hesitates, then drinks the pills.

Right, stand up. Here, take my hand. She pulls him to his feet. Show me. She gestures to his genitals.

You are not going to inject there! No. Luzoko exclaims, horrified.

No, no, the injections are for your bum. She slips the headlight onto her head, and switches it on. I must also clean the germs on the outside. He hesitates. You've already broken the rule, so now let's do this properly. Let me clean the wound.

She's going for a professional tone to mask her discomfort. It is possible for initiates to lose their penises to gangrene, and she needs to see how bad this is, while not wanting to look at all. The last time she saw Luzoko's penis, he was five years old and running naked through the sprinkler on the lawn in the heat. He lifts the edge of his blanket, intensifying an acrid smell. Two thin, muscular legs smeared with white clay, then the mess of his sex. The shaft of his penis looks as though the man who wielded the knife has cut off too much skin, or else the terrible swelling makes it seem so, but there is a defect above the glans which is red and raw, full of slough and pus.

Kate pours a dash of antiseptic into the mug of hot water, then tests it with her finger to make sure it has cooled sufficiently. She hands it to him, hoping he did not see the shock and disgust in her face. Put it in there, she instructs.

Slowly, gingerly, he immerses his wound in the antiseptic solution, gasping and grunting with pain. Kate takes a syringe and removes the protective cap. Turn round. Now, keep still. She sticks the needle into his buttock muscle and depresses the plunger. Not a flinch.

She waits, to see whether he has a reaction to the first dose. You okay?

Shoot, he orders.

How long does one wait? Sweat pricks her armpits. This is why one needs to go to medical school.

Nothing happens.

I'm fine. Do it.

Second syringe. Insert the needle. Again she injects, and it is done.

She finds the packet of gauze swabs in the basket. Let me see, she says. He lowers the mug and Kate bends forward, focussing the headlight onto the wound. She wets the swab and, as carefully as she can, wipes away the pus, wishing she had gloves. Kate has to hold the root of his penis to keep the appendage still enough. Luzoko tenses against the pain as the flesh beneath springs little leaks of blood, so she loses courage and soon stops. She squeezes antibiotic cream out onto a piece of gauze and smears it over the wound.

There. Kate straightens up. She has had enough dramas with men's penises for today.

Luzoko pulls his blanket around him. Thank you, Miss Kate. Enkosi kakhulu. You have done a good thing. I will be fine now.

She puts a hand on his shoulder, the heat still radiating through. Take care, she says, wanting to say so much more to this son, this child, this man; so afraid of him taking his leave of her, perhaps of his life. Sleep here tonight, Kate offers, but he shakes his head, anxious to go.

I'm fine, he insists. Much better already. They both know he is lying.

Let me drive you back. Luzoko shakes his head. He cannot afford to be seen in Kate's bakkie.

Take this. Kate holds out the packet of food. Ham and cheese.

He shakes his head again. Thank you, it is enough.

She remembers he is not permitted meat or milk products until his circumcision has healed. Well, at least take this, Kate gives him the jar of Vaseline. For your lips. There'll be a time when you'll feel like kissing a woman again.

He returns her smile, dips his finger into the gel and applies a little around his mouth.

I might be going away tomorrow and I'm very worried about you. If you're not a bit better by midday, it means the antibiotics are not working. You must promise me that you'll go to the clinic.

He nods, his hand already on the door knob, his eyes averted.

Luzoko, Kate warns him, if you keep this promise, I won't tell your mother what happened here tonight.

He nods again, then he is gone.

Kate steps outside, wanting to run after him and fold him into her arms. But the young man has already disappeared into the night. She clears up and pours the infected contents of the mug onto the ground outside the hok – a libation to the goddess of healing. Nausea stirs in her belly.

I have done what I can, she consoles herself.

Carry on down the path that draws her feet towards the house, towards sleep. No sound from the owls now. So few left. Perhaps she dreamt the owl hoot this morning. Rattex should be banned.

Her heart warms with the thought that there is at least one young person who trusts her, who finds her good enough – a good-enough mother.

Any decent mother would've taken him to hospital, she falters.

Other mothers will have taken care of Jess today, the church women, the hospital staff. There are other women who understand her daughter in ways she does not.

Every moment in life presents a judgement call, she muses. She has been so critical of Jess's choices, yet her own have often been suspect. Options present themselves every minute of every day. How to take the right path. To eat this food or to refuse. Agree to have sex with this person or not. Acquiesce to this person's bad behaviour or object. Walk away or towards, stay or leave. Cut the neural tissue here, or cut it there. Accede to Luzoko's request or not. Catch a plane tomorrow, or another day, or never. Each bifurcation splitting a life into what was and was not chosen, wittingly or unwittingly.

Kate thinks of all those multiple potential and discarded lives lying behind her, blown away like husks, leaving her with only this one that she strides on down to the next decision. All the choices she has made that day, that year, during her whole life, all of them have led her here, to this path leading her across the field back to the home of her childhood.

Inside the back door, Kate kicks off her boots and shuffles on her slippers. Deposits the swabs and mug into the bin. Washes her hands thoroughly at the laundry sink, incanting: Luzoko will be healed and all will be well. Storm will be healed and all will be well. Jess will be healed and all will be well. I will be healed and all will be well. Spinning a cocoon to enfold and soothe her.

Nine fifty-seven. The house is silent. Her urgent need is to lie down. But she is filthy and thirsty. While the kettle boils, she runs a bath to wash away this day from hell.

Not a creak or a moan from upstairs.

Pours the water onto the teabag. The house is much too silent. Fetches the milk, squeezes the teabag out and takes the brew through to the bathroom. Turns the taps off.

Listens to the silence. Kate goes quickly up the stairs. Her father has hit his head; perhaps she has taken it too lightly. She and her father should swap bedrooms before he falls down the stairs, but she fears that any disruption to his routine could cause him to lose what few bearings he has.

Da's bedroom door is unlocked. Light falls into the room as she opens it slowly. Elihle's single bed in a corner is empty. Where are they? she panics. But a snuffled grunt reveals Da in his bed. Elihle is sitting quietly next to her father with a placating hand on his shoulder. He looks up at Kate and puts a forefinger to his lips.

Kate closes the door softly, and stands on the landing, overwhelmed.

Elihle, Nosisi has explained to Kate, means the beautiful one. One whose parents thought he would gain from the promise of a new South Africa which arrived when he was a small boy. The one who has been betrayed by the new dispensation. The one who has minimal education, and whose parents died for lack of basic health care.

Elihle is lucky to have this job, having only reached standard five. But he cannot live this life, too close as it is to slavery. She pays Elihle a good enough wage, enough that he does not consider going to work at the saw mill where his parents had been employed before they died. Elihle may be beautiful, but he is not lucky.

Kate wonders what it will take for meaningful change to come to this country. The slow laying down of new neural pathways in a million different brains towards a peaceful ending? Or will it be swift and bloody, with the saintly patience of people like Elihle and Nosisi finally running out, their muscles filling with rage? Their No resounding, their eyes resistant. The beaches are open to all people now, and you can sleep with or marry whoever you like. Hundreds of racist laws have been repealed, and a small influential group of black people have been assisted into middle-class status with the introduction of BEE, acting as ballast. But Kate knows: The privileged minority are still sailing on the deck of the old ship, the galley slaves grinding away below, keeping things going without any real say as to where this country is heading, and how it might get there.

Downstairs, Kate's bath water is growing cold. She descends, closes the bathroom door behind her, and strips. The present remains consistently present, while the future tickertapes through to the past. Here comes the end bracket. Her death is on its way to greet her. Each day is precious, each day is a single page of a life story.

Today is a page she wants to tear out and set alight.

Kate ties back her hair, steps into the bath and sinks slowly into the thrill of hot water, down and in, up to her chin, her body shivering with delight. Strange purse of flesh, this body we inhabit, she thinks. What a foreign language it speaks, with its aches and flushes and tics. How to understand it, this body she is calling 'it', but which is also herself. This body that will increasingly disobey her as she grows older.

Despite all hardships, she does not want to be separated from this life.

Cinnamon soap, made by Nosisi's friend from the village, slips in her hand. Its fragrance displaces some pain with a lift of pleasure.

Storm will be healed and all will be well. Luzoko

will be healed and all will be well.

Kate sighs. In a hundred years' time nobody will know or care how she'd lived or died. No one will remember her. She will have been buried alongside her parents at the far corner of the farm, her flesh blurring into and merging with the eternal landscape through the action of worms and bacteria, her bones loosening their connections, falling apart.

There will be a funeral. She wonders whether Jess's church goes for simple ceremonies, or lavish morbid dramas. When Kate dies, she wants to be fed back into the ground to the soundtrack of Mozart's Requiem. A yellowwood planted over her while her friends crack open some good wine. She'd like to come back as yellowwood, her arms branching into the sky, her feet rooted deeply. She'd like to be home to a thousand little creatures.

It is clear: She couldn't love the twins in case they died. *Children should not die.* She could hardly touch them. Jessica could see that, and could not forgive her.

She will go over to London and learn how to love. If she can set aside her anger and access her grief, if she can choose to sit still for long enough to get to know and appreciate Storm, if she can learn when to speak and when to stay silent, perhaps her daughter will forgive her.

Time to top up the hot water, or to dry herself and get to bed. Kate is almost asleep in the dreamy deep. Soap the armpits, feet, nether bits. Gulp tea down. Delicious tea, her senses are returning. Pull the plug, squat, releasing her urine to join the outflow. Rinse, now rise. A good hard towel to dry her back. Between the toes, her back twinging. Dry her sex.

What was that burning compulsion that seized me? she wonders. Now there is nothing except the desire to fold herself in sleep.

Kate wraps the towel around her and goes to the bedroom, where the dogs are already lying on their blankets. They lift their great heads, tails thumping a greeting. On her bedside table, on top of the pile of recommended books she never gets round to reading, lies the envelope. Leonard's gesture. Kindness, manipulation, revenge, restitution.

Luzoko was crystal clear about what he wanted from her.

She hangs the towel up on a hook at the back of the door and slides into bed between cool sheets. Her body is grateful to be quiet at last.

Kate switches off the bedside light; darkness fills the room.

The cheese rounds she has created are lying in the dark of the cellar, the micro-organisms busily transforming what she has set in motion and now must leave alone, trusting and waiting. They are evidence of her life, of her life's work. So much other work to do – she has to pack, and write instructions for Nosisi and Gert. Ask Daniel to do the shopping. Flour and onions. Check the pantry. She needs to leave the house before lunchtime. She cannot remember how many guests are booked tomorrow. Nosisi is more than capable of running the restaurant, she is grateful for that, but Kate will have to look Nosisi in the eye in the morning as she discusses the arrangements, and somehow keep her promise.

The antibiotic, filtering into Luzuko's blood stream tonight, this too she has set in motion, trusting that it will do its work and that all will be well.

She must assume that Luzoko will also keep his word and go to the clinic if he gets worse. She cannot betray him, yet mothers cannot stand by and do nothing. She will consult her dreams, the oldest of oracles. Last night, she could not save Jess from drowning. Even in her dream she felt paralysed. Her inability to act is why it took her so long to leave Leonard. She is an endurer, a boarding school survivor, accepting a situation long after she should have cut loose, with no certainty about where, or how, or whether she will land.

There was an owl, for certain. Kate listens, and there it is again, the softest hoot. One of the last survivors on a human-infested planet. One who watches over the night. Perhaps she is a sign, sent by her ancestors.

May she eat only natural, uncontaminated rats tonight. May she live to a ripe old owl age.

Tomorrow …

Acknowledgements

Thank you to Ken Barris, John Cartwright, Veronica Cecil, Alje van Deemter, Robert Hamblin, Giles Griffiths, Jacqui L'Ange, Sindiwe Magona, John Maytham, Karin Schimke, Catherine Shepherd, Nobesuthu Tom and Erika Viljoen for reading and commenting on drafts of the manuscript. Thanks to Alje van Deemter who allowed me to job shadow him on his farm Fynboshoek in the Eastern Cape so that I could detail his cheese-making process and restaurant business – his produce is as delicious as the book portrays. To Katy McLean for her sensitive depiction of my novel in her artwork. Heartfelt thanks to Karina M. Szczurek, my editor and publisher, for recognising and supporting my work.